C000007807

FALTER

THE NASH BROTHERS, BOOK FOUR

CARRIE AARONS

Copyright © 2019 by Carrie Aarons

All rights reserved.

No part of this book may be reproduced in any form or by any electronic or mechanical means, including information storage and retrieval systems, without written permission from the author, except for the use of brief quotations in a book review.

This is a work of fiction. Names, characters, businesses, places, events and incidents are either the products of the author's imagination or used in a fictitious manner. Any resemblance to actual persons, living or dead, or actual events is purely coincidental.

Editing done by Proofing Style.

Cover designed by Okay Creations.

Do you want your **FREE** Carrie Aarons eBook?

All you have to do is **<u>sign up for my newsletter</u>**, and you'll immediately receive your free book!

1

RYAN

Dust settles as the propellers of the small plane die down, forcing me to cover my mouth with my free hand.

The "airport" is anything but the traditional sense of the word. I'm used to international hubs of travel, teeming with people speaking different languages and jostling for a prime spot in the security line. When I think of runways, I think of intricate loops of lighted flight paths, the whole design like a mini-city in itself.

But, just like everything else in this small town, the airport is a teaspoon of what I consider normal.

The last time I stepped foot in Fawn Hill, Pennsylvania was two years ago when I'd been helping Forrest Nash solve a case. It feels strange to be back now, having just exited a puddle jumper on the dirt runway outside the solitary building I assume houses the sparsely manned air traffic control and baggage claim teams.

I'm a little older, not really any wiser, and am sporting a broken heart for the ages. When Presley suggested I come out for a visit after my last relationship flamed out in spectacular fashion, I was wary.

Something about this little town ingrains itself in you. Makes you want to be kinder, more intimate with the humans that surround you day-to-day, to not take life so seriously, or live it as fast as the people whose circles I run in do.

That scares the bejesus out of me. I've never had a proper family or let anyone in as thoroughly as the residents of this town do. You could know someone here for mere minutes, and they were inviting you in for a meal. It took me almost a year to trust Presley back when I first met her, and we were living together for some of that time.

For someone like me, with what I've been through, trust and loyalty never came easy.

It was mindboggling, then, how I kept ending up in the crappiest of relationships. I'm sure some therapist out there would cite some study that said I had daddy, and mommy, issues. That I craved a partner who could take care of me, that even in the wrong situation, I'd stayed a prolonged period of time before throwing in the towel.

This hypothetical therapist might be right, but it didn't mean I'd stopped getting myself into these dead-on-arrival romances. Well, until now.

No boyfriends, no lovers, no men of any kind barking up my tree for a year. That was the deal I made with myself, and I was sticking to it.

"Oh my God, you're here!"

Presley runs at me at full speed, throwing her arms around me and almost lifting me off the ground even though I have four inches on her.

"Jeez, Pres, you're going to make me even more nauseous than that plane ride did." I laugh, but hug her back, resting my chin on the top of her head while my feet dangle just above the ground.

I met Presley almost a decade ago when we were both practically infants struggling to live in New York City. Most weeks, we'd have to choose between eating and running the air-conditioning unit shoved into one of our apartment windows. And when I say apartment, I mean shoebox you could walk across in two seconds flat. But that struggle made us closer, and she's the person I trust most in life.

When her grandmother could no longer look after the bookstore in Fawn Hill that had been in their family for generations, Presley moved here to help. Not long after that, my red-headed gypsy met Keaton Nash and his merry band of brothers. She and the town sweetheart slash hot veterinarian fell in love, got married, and are now Mr. and Mrs. Fawn Hill, basically.

Over the years, I've visited on and off. I've gotten to befriend Presley's sisters-in-law, Lily and Penelope, and their husbands, Bowen and Forrest. Eliza their mother, is always kind when I come to town, as is Hattie, Presley's grandmother.

My best friend sets me down and holds my arms out to the sides to inspect me. "It's just been so long since I've seen you. A whole year, you Grecian, you. Have you lost weight? You were living in Santorini for a year and didn't put on one pound from all that baklava?"

Her words are teasing, but I can see the concern in her eyes. I duck my head. "Believe me, I ate enough for a small army. But the past month has been ... trying ..."

What I'm trying to say is that it's hard to eat when your relationship is disintegrating in front of your eyes.

"Well, no matter. Eliza cooked about a billion trays of casseroles and lasagnas for Lily and Bowen after the baby arrived, so we'll steal some of those."

She loops my arm in hers and begins escorting me toward the doorless Jeep waiting on the side of the building.

"Oh, I can't wait to see Lily and that rugrat! She's probably the cutest thing in the world. Hey, is this a new car?" I ask, throwing my bags into the open-air trunk and then grabbing the roll bar to lift myself into the passenger seat.

Presley's red ponytail glints in the summer sun, and I'm surprised to find that I miss the muggy hotness of the East Coast.

"I bought it for myself after I hit my financial goals at the studio." She grins shyly, announcing her success but not boasting about it.

My hand comes up to punch her shoulder gently. "Pres! How awesome, I'm so proud of you!"

"Thanks." She smiles, starting the engine.

I'm glad our conversation is ended with the noise of the wind and bounce of the Jeep as we drive over the country dirt roads. It gives me a minute to bask in the sunshine, to breathe in the air of an America in July, to relish the complete, untethered freedom I have right now. The crushing sadness that has sat heavy on my heart for the past couple of weeks begins to ease. It's incredible how wholly one can lose themselves when trying to love another person with everything they have. It's even more terrifically awful how much more they'll give when the effort being returned is less than zero.

I've never thought of myself as that girl, but as an adult, all I've done is abandon my identity when a new man comes along.

Presley turns the Jeep onto a paved road, the car slowing as I spot houses in the distance. Her typical uniform of yoga pants and a tank top looks much more comfortable than my jeans and short-sleeved sweater, which are now sticking to me in sweaty, hot patches. I don't know what I was thinking, traveling in such an outfit. Maybe I'd yearned for the cool wardrobe of a Manhattanite, when in all reality, I was going to be in the sticks for the foreseeable future.

"You needed to get off the grid," Presley says, almost as if she's reading my thoughts.

I nod, staring out the front windshield. "I'm not sure you even know how much."

"I'm here when you're ready." My best friend knows me too well.

Shrugging, my small smile is directed at her. "Thanks, but you already know the gist. Same old when it comes to my love life. Can't seem to get it right. Hey, maybe Keaton has a brother."

My joke sends a grin turning up Presley's lips. Because he has three ... two of which are taken. All the Nash men are equally strapping, smart, and reliable in their own way.

And the only one left just happens to be the one who makes my lungs stop working whenever I see him.

Just then, as if I've conjured him by imagination, a figure running in the direction of our car appears over the horizon line on the road.

Pure male adrenaline jogging toward us at a steady pace. A body well over six feet ... I know this because tiny chills have run down my spine when we've stood next to each other and I've been forced to look up. Tanned skin slicked with sweat stretched over taut, wiry muscle, with thick, athletic thighs pumping rhythmically as he pounds the pavement.

Fletcher Nash, in the flesh. Of course, the second person I run into in Fawn Hill is the one man I should be actively staying away from.

One year, I'd promised myself.

So why, in the first two seconds of spotting him in the zone during a workout, do I want to throw every new principle I've adopted right out the window?

As he nears, our eyes connect, and a flicker of recognition runs over his face. I feel the world go full-on slow-motion, with Fletcher's steps slowing and the tires on the car all but coming to a stop. Those blue eyes, the color of the sea outside my window in Santorini, blink twice, and his tongue darts out to wet his lips.

He's all hard lines and lean control, and I often wonder what he was like before he stopped drinking.

It's more than just physical attraction between us, though. I've never been alone in a room with Fletcher, and yet, I can tell that he and I are the same. He knows next to nothing about my past, but when he looks at me, I feel as if he understands the pain inside my chest.

Presley honks violently, snapping me out of my trance, waving her free hand out the window in a furious greeting of her brother-in-law. Fletcher raises a hand, waving back, and smiling with all the pearly whites in his mouth showing.

"You go, bro!" Presley yells as we pass him, her brother-in-law not stopping his run to chat with us.

I can't help it when my head swivels backward, staring at his retreating form as those perfectly sculpted calves carry him over the hot pavement.

"He runs six miles every morning. Told me once that it helps with the cravings," my best friend divulges.

The last thing I need is temptation, especially in the form of a recovering addict who would never be able to give me the kind of support I'd need in a relationship.

So, I turn back around and root myself firmly forward in my seat.

No good will come from ogling Fletcher Nash, even if I have a hard time shutting down the thoughts racing through my head.

2

The itch in the back of my throat is so strong, that it takes everything in my body to even sit up in bed.

No, this itch is not physical, it's not something you can clear with a drink of water or a cough drop. This irritating feeling, a throb that cannot be shooed out of your brain with a silly distraction like song lyrics, is bone deep ... it sits in the marrow.

The itch is addiction, and even after almost five years of sobriety, I wake up each day with the overwhelming urge to drink. To drown myself in a bottle of cheap tequila, or my favorite IPA, or the crisp hard cider that Mr. Hinard makes on his orchard just over the county line.

I can name you almost every brand of vodka in the liquor store next to the pizza place on Main Street. Not because I've stepped foot in there in five years, but because in the ten years before that, I could have checked in like it was a long-term-stay hotel I frequented.

To push past the cravings takes every ounce of energy in my body. I have to literally latch my hands behind my back to keep them from grabbing my keys and heading out in search of a buzz.

That's the thing no one can quite explain when you go through rehab and start attending meetings. They say it will be hard, that your sobriety is essential to living a healthy life, that if you stop drinking, everything will turn around. Counselors tell you to focus on the positive and surround yourself with people who live a life you aspire to have. Other recovering alcoholics warn about the dangers of social situations and the reality of wronged friends not accepting you as a sober person, even if you make amends.

But I'm not sure anyone told me how crippling the feeling of addiction would be. That even years later, almost half a decade, I'd still wake up with a lump in my throat and my hands shaking to grip a bottle. When they say you're an addict for life, even after getting sober, they mean it.

Stumbling to the bathroom, I lock the door before taking my morning piss. Living with your mother at the age of twenty-nine is not only embarrassing but having her walk in on you mid-drawer drop is something I'll never quite scrub from my brain.

Note to all kids out there; stay in school, don't do drugs and lay off the bottle. Otherwise, you'll end up living with your mom, working a dead-end job, and trying to rebuild your life as a grown-ass man.

After I drain the snake, I wash my hands, brush my teeth, and head back to the spare bedroom in my mom's condo that has been mine ever since I got back from rehab. As if being the baby of four brothers didn't come with enough teasing, I'd now put myself in the position to be called pathetic.

I try not to berate myself, as I do each time I walk into a house that isn't my own, as I dress for my daily run.

Six miles, every single morning. Endorphins help with the

cravings and you don't have much time to think with heavy metal blasting in your ears and your feet pounding the road.

"Do you want some coffee?" Mom asks as I enter the kitchen, sitting in her usual chair at the table in the breakfast nook.

I shake my head. "No, thanks. Just my usual goo before my run."

All I eat before my workouts is one of those disgusting gel packets that make me shudder just thinking about it. The goop is gross sliding down your throat but it fills your stomach without making you want to vomit halfway through and gives you enough energy to not have me passing out after six miles in the hot July sun.

"Can you pick up milk on your way home? We're almost out." Her attention is back on the local paper splayed out in front of her.

"Sure. See you in a bit," I tell her, kissing her on the cheek and heading for the front door.

The heat blasts me in the face as soon as I step outside. It's summer days now, which means that even at seven thirty in the morning, it's a balmy seventy-five. Not that I mind, the harder I sweat, the more the itch in the back of my throat lessens.

Before slipping my phone into the arm band strapped around my right bicep, I scroll through my music to the heavy metal playlist I compiled. Hitting shuffle, an Iron Maiden song blasts through my headphones, giving my heart a jolt akin to an electric shock. Blood begins pumping furiously into my loins, the excitement and fear of a long, hard run mixing in a heady combination.

My muscles scream as I run, trying to beat the pace I set yesterday. That's how my life goes; I'm always trying to do a little better than I did yesterday. So far, I haven't backslid much, which I'm thankful for.

I'm also so far behind every other person my age, there probably isn't any deeper to sink.

I spot Presley's new white open-top Jeep the minute I come up over the hill. My sister-in-law might be a free-spirit, rolling meadows kind of girl, but she's still got some of that New York City extra-ness in her that our small town just can't erase. The truck is flashy, with all the bells and whistles, and I honestly love it. Bowen grumbled about how obnoxious it was when she bought it, and of course, my twin brother's wife, Penelope, sat on top of the roll bar the day Presley and Keaton pulled up to Mom's in it.

There is someone in the passenger seat, I notice, as my sneakers push rhythmically off the hot blacktop. It's strange that Presley would be out here at this time of day ... nothing leads from this road but the airport.

The airport ... which means the person in her passenger seat is ...

Ryan Shea.

As the truck slows, and my sister-in-law begins wildly waving her hand at me, I study the woman sitting next to her.

She looks different from the last time I saw her, more than two years ago. Her raven-black hair is longer, past her shoulders, where it used to be styled in a short cut that made her look like a punk rock princess. Ryan looks thinner, a fact I'm concerned about even if I haven't seen her in years. She still has the same dark and mysterious personality, like she might kiss you one second and throw you down a well the next. Her amber eyes, the color of smooth whiskey, connect immediately with mine.

And even though I'm already sweating my balls off, being within her vicinity makes me feel as if the sun instantly started burning a thousand degrees hotter.

The first time I met her was at Presley and Keaton's wedding, when they were trying to set her up with my twin brother.

Forrest and Ryan are both hackers, or coders depending on who you talk to. While my brother now worked with local law enforcement to catch cyber criminals, Ryan was a consultant. She took jobs all around the world with different companies, protecting their data and testing their computer forensic weaknesses. Her life is glamorous and expensive, whereas mine is as cheap and rundown as the motel out on the outskirts of town.

Swiftly, I avert my gaze, because I know that if I look too long, I'll start to want things I can't give her.

When I got sober, I made a vow to myself that I wouldn't be with another woman until it was the real deal. I wouldn't touch another female until the relationship was so serious, I was thinking about making her my wife.

After years of blacking out night after night, ending up asleep in bushes, or on couches at houses where I woke up and didn't know a single soul ... it was a miracle I wasn't dead, riddled with STDs, or in debt to five baby mamas. It might sound ridiculous, but it's true; I don't remember a single sexual encounter for the last almost ten years of my life because of how fucked up I'd been.

Ryan Shea ... she's the type of temptation that I need to avoid at all costs.

She's the type of woman who could make all of those cravings slam right back into my throat.

She's the exact type to become an addiction. And that means talking to her, looking at her, hell ... even breathing in her direction.

It's all off limits.

3

"**Y**ou're sure you wouldn't be more comfortable in the guest room?"

Presley eyes me as I unpack the bigger of my two bags.

I shake my head. "No, I want you two to have your privacy. Plus, if I have any hysterical crying fits, it'll be nicer not to have Keaton hear them."

My best friend chews her lip as a frown of worry marks her pretty, freckled face. "Ry, I'm not going to rush you, but just promise me you're not as bad as you seem?"

Does she want me to tell her that I'm not suicidal? Because I'm not. Though, I am so heartbroken and damaged, that someone like Presley couldn't understand. My best friend, although I love her, can be a bit dramatic about being the outcast of her family. And now that she's been all about worshipped by the Nash clan, she feels a type of compassion that I will never experience.

Because while other people have at least *one person* they can turn to if all else fails, I have no one. I was raised in the New York state foster system, bouncing from house to house until I was eighteen and could finally, legally, make decisions for myself. I was an orphan, my only living relative was my biological mother who ... the damage she'd done was something that can never be forgotten.

Shaking my head to clear it, I paste on a smile. "I'll be okay. I'm better now that I'm here, okay? Now will you go inside and kiss your adorable husband and stop worrying about me?"

"Fine. But there is so much food in the fridge, I wasn't sure if you were still eating meat or not. So I stocked up on everything I know you like, including those disgusting chocolate Twizzlers. Come into the house whenever you like, and I have a yoga class at three that has your name on it."

It's kind of sweet that she prepared things for me, and I know it's to keep my mind off my breakup with Yanis. Ugh, just thinking his name makes my heart surge with fury, regret, and sorrow.

"Thanks. You're a really good friend. Even after I went distant for a few years ..."

"Don't even mention it." Presley shushes me, enveloping me in a big bear hug. "All right, I'll see you at the studio. It's not a far walk, but if you want a ride, there are plenty of Nashes around to give you one."

With that, she leaves me alone in her shed turned guest cottage. I turn in a circle, marveling at how far down the bottom of the barrel I've sunk. I used to live in Manhattan, the greatest city in the world. Two weeks ago, I woke up to a cerulean blue ocean and white-washed houses built into the side of a mountain in Santorini.

Now, I live in my best friend's backyard, in the middle of small-town Pennsylvania. Not that the cottage didn't have its own charm, with all the modern fixings. It just wasn't Positano or Berlin.

I sound like a spoiled brat. I know that; I do ... it's just, I can't help but feel sorry for myself. I feel lost, untethered, and without a purpose in my own life. Never in my thirty-one years have I felt like that. When you grow up with nothing, it almost fuels you. To be better, to become the best, to succeed. No one tells you what happens when you get everything you strived for, but it feels all wrong.

My suitcases on the bed beg to be unpacked, and although it'll make this situation more permanent, I am not the type of person to leave their stuff in bags for weeks. The work will occupy my hands and mind, at least for a little while.

The guest cottage is a studio of sorts, a decently sized room with a queen bed, oversized chair, dresser, small closet and mini-fridge. There is a tiny TV on top of the dresser, and an adjoining bathroom that's no bigger than a coffin ... but at least I won't have to go into the house to pee and shower.

For this moment in time, it's just what I need. And provides privacy that a guest room inside of Presley and Keaton's home never could.

When everything is put away, I check the time on my cell phone. One fifteen in the afternoon. Just enough time for me to raid Presley's fridge, throw on yoga clothes, and walk to the studio. Unlike the people in Fawn Hill, I'm used to walking everywhere. I haven't owned a car in seven years; my feet and public transportation have been my modes of travel.

"Aw, yeahhhh." I pump a fist in the air when I spot the homemade turkey burgers in the refrigerator.

I grab one, a slice of cheese, a pickle, and some sweet potato fries I find in another container. Keaton Nash really knows the way to a girl's heart, even if it isn't his wife's. When the food is warm, I take it out back and eat on the patio, basking in the scorching summer heat.

My cell phone dings on the table top, a notification from my Facebook app chiming.

Opening the social media network, I scroll for a minute before I check the notification. Turns out, it's actually a message from ...

Yanis.

I curse myself for not blocking him on all of my social media profiles, but I've sort of been traveling as fast as I can to get away from him, so ...

Deleting the message without reading it, I flip over to my email. I'm sure this new message from him doesn't say anything different than the twenty texts, emails and voicemails he's already left me.

Before I can convince myself not to, I stupidly open my voicemail and play the most recent message from him.

"*My beauty, please come back to me. You know I love you more than a thousand suns. We Europeans are freer than Americans, I miss my glamour girl.*"

Rolling my eyes, I hit delete in a fit of rage. And then carrying that fury with me, I erase every single message, email and correspondence he's ever sent me. Our relationship is so over, it's buried deeper than the ships at the bottom of the sea surrounding Santorini.

The bastard, with his Greek god body, rolling accent, carefree charm and flowery language. I should have seen right through his bullshit, but just like every other time I've fallen in love, I ignored every warning sign.

Which is probably why I found him, a year and a half into our relationship, screwing not one but *two* skanks in our bed.

I need a distraction. Checking the time, I see I've wasted enough to be comfortably early to Presley's yoga class, and quickly throw on my clothes and walk over to the studio.

Being away for so long, I'd forgotten how charming Fawn Hill's main street is. It's everything you picture when you think of a small town, with some newer shops thrown in. One of those is Presley's business.

"Ryan! I didn't know you were in town," Lily greets me as I walk.

I hug her, honestly amazed that she looks so thin for just having had a baby a month ago. "Um, I'm sorry, did you even pop a kid out?"

She chuckles. "An eight pounder! She's so cute, but, and I feel guilty saying this, I love my afternoons off when Bowen watches her. Getting a class in here and there helps me relax."

Blinking, I still can't stop staring at her. As if Lily Nash wasn't already the sweetest, most perfect person I've ever met ... of course, she looks like a damn model after pregnancy.

"So, how are you? You've been in, wait don't remind me ... Italy?" She taps a finger to her nose.

"Greece," I say, quickly changing the subject. "How is mom life?"

Lily's face turns into an adorable mushy expression of love. "It is so amazing. I feel like I could cry at the drop of a hat just thinking about her."

And sure enough, she begins to tear up. Presley comes over, her face flushed, from what I assume has been her day of teaching and pats her sister-in-law on the shoulder.

"Are you crying again?" Her expression is sympathetic.

Lily nods and retreats to the bathroom to dab her eyes.

"Did you eat?" Presley asks, that note of concern still in her voice.

"Yes, *Mom*." I roll my eyes. "Pres, I appreciate all you're doing, but I don't need a babysitter. I'm going to be okay. I can feed and clothe myself, and I'll figure out how to heal in my own time. I love you."

I squeeze her hand and she manages a small smile.

"All right, well let's work some of those issues out on the mat. Time for class."

The yoga class is an intense hour of stretching, holding, balancing and deep thinking ... something I'm very thankful for. It takes me out of my body, numbs my mind for a while so that the thoughts buzzing around in there don't drown me in anxiety.

Afterward, I feel this kind of cathartic need to almost ... cry, maybe? I haven't cried since I found Yanis cheating on me. Not when I packed up my shit, not when I hopped on a plane, and not even when I touched down in the US.

Quickly, I throw a wave Presley's way and exit the studio. She must have some inkling not to run after me, because I walk home in silence, just letting all the emotions run over me like the tide.

My muscles yelp with soreness, but in a good way. It's been a while since I had a good, centered yoga practice ... it was something Presley got me into when we lived in New York. But since moving away, and becoming so involved with my ex-boyfriend, I put a lot of my interests on hold.

It feels good to get back to what I used to love.

The shower does me good, working the hot water over my aching body, and I take my time lathering and breathing in the steam.

When I'm done, I apply my moisturizer, deodorant, and body lotion. I'm nothing if not a stickler for routine.

I exit the tiny bathroom, a towel wrapped around my wet hair and not a stitch of clothing on my dewy, bare skin.

So it's no wonder I squawk like a frightened bird when Fletcher Nash walks into my accommodations, causing every muscle in my body to freeze as his eyes lick a hot, wanton trail down my naked flesh.

4

After my shift at the grocery store, where I've been working as a cashier since before I got sober, I drive across town.

Mom's shower head in her master bathroom is leaking again, and I told her I'd fix it two days ago. She, and the rest of my family, have already done too much ... it will take me the rest of my lifetime to pay them back. So over to Keaton's I go, to borrow his toolbox.

Keaton and Presley aren't home when I pull into the driveway, of course. Those two barely ever occupy the same space these days, what with her studio and his animal patients. It works for them, both of them whole people on their own who happen to love each other beyond reason. I admire that kind of companionship, that kind of dedication. It's what I want in a partner ... if I ever find one worthy.

Not of me, hell, a sewer rat would be classier and more noble than the woman I deserve to end up with. But, I mean worthy of climbing over the speed bump I've set up for myself.

Visions of Ryan in the passenger seat of Presley's Jeep fill my thoughts, and I push them away. I walk to their fridge, pulling out a pitcher of lemonade I'm sure Keaton made, and not Presley. He's the better cook of the two.

The cool, tart drink hits my throat and my temper instantly cools, my hackles having been up for the past eight hours. The shifts at the grocery store were getting old ... *really* old. Dealing with asshole customers, ringing up item after item in an assembly line of boredom, biting my tongue when the dickhead of a manager makes some snide comment. We went to high school together and now he holds a position of power, albeit a pathetic one, over me and relishes it to no end.

Just a couple more years, I think to myself. I've been squirreling away money and living with Mom helps. I've had a few decent commissioned pieces from buyers, and I hope that someday, my woodworking can serve as my only source of income. For now, though, I'm not getting bigger than my britches.

It's all a process, to attain the life I really want. And yes, I've been listening to self-help podcasts ... that shit helps sometimes.

Going in search of the toolbox, I walk outside and into the converted shed. My brother and sister-in-law made it a guest house of sorts when they thought I was going to move in with them for a while. It didn't work out that way; I feel more needed at Mom's and want to repay my debt to society, but it's still good if someone needs to crash.

The minute I walk through the French doors, whose shades I didn't realize were drawn until after the fact, every bit of lust in the atmosphere slams into me like a bullet train.

Standing in the middle of the studio-like guest cottage is Ryan Shea.

Completely naked save for a towel wrapped around her head.

I might go into cardiac arrest, that's how hard my heart is pumping. It has been a long time since I've seen a naked woman in the flesh, my computer helps me out with the simulated part.

The fact that this woman is slender but curvy, olive skin stretching across all of those hidden, erotic places ...

The fact that this woman is Ryan ... my throat dries up in seconds, and my cock goes from zero to midnight in a flash.

Her pussy is bare of any hair, and I long to sink to my knees and plant a kiss between her perfect thighs. My eyes travel up to her breasts, full and supple, her budded nipples the shade of a dark rose. The scents of vanilla and citrus waft through the air, and suddenly, I want to unwrap the towel and see if that smell lingers in her hair.

Finally, our eyes lock, her face free of any makeup, but then again, a woman as gorgeous as this doesn't need any. She lets me look at her, unabashed, for another moment.

"I'm so sorry." I let out a sharp hiss, jumping to turn away.

I can hear Ryan fumbling behind me, probably reaching for some clothing. "*Oh my God.*"

"I didn't know you were staying in here, or with Presley and Keaton at all. Fuck, I'm a moron, of course, you're staying here. I just mean, I didn't mean to barge in on you ..."

The rambling won't stop, and I can't seem to stop picturing her naked body. The mental image is burned into the front of my brain, and I know it will be the number one called upon memory in my spank bank for a long time to come.

"Looking for your athlete's foot cream, again?" She chuckles at my turned back.

If she were looking at me dead in the face, she'd see the furious blush working its way over my cheeks. "Thankfully, I don't have that problem anymore."

I am a damn liar. I still have athlete's foot, a result of constant running. I'm surprised she remembers that embarrassing moment when I walked into Forrest's house years ago, asking for the medicinal cream, and she'd been sitting on his couch.

"Well, I guess we're both even on the embarrassment front," I manage to choke out.

There is a *pssh* sound from behind me. "This is way more embarrassing than you asking for foot cream! You saw me naked!"

My fingers won't stop moving, tapping on my legs and wringing themselves in the other hand. I drop my head, unable to stop the words from rushing out of my mouth.

"There is nothing embarrassing about this, Ryan. Other than the fact that I walked in without knocking. But your body? Seeing you naked ... I assure you, there is nothing humiliating about it. I've thought about this for a long time. Probably too often, if I'm being honest. Which, I guess, since we're getting down to the bare bones of it, I have to be. You're absolutely beautiful, every part of you. I only wish I had more time to examine every dip and crevice that makes you up. I apologize for surprising you, it won't happen again."

My lungs burn with the words I shouldn't have let out, and I'm too much of a coward to turn around and face her before I bolt for the exit.

"Can we slow down a bit? I'm winded, gosh, do I feel out of shape."

Lily pushes the stroller with baby Molly in it, some paces behind Presley and me. Penelope is trying to wrangle Ames, her youngest son, from jumping in a pond fully clothed, and I have to smile at how much adulting we're doing.

"You just had a baby, give yourself some grace," Penelope chides her best friend as we all fall into step together.

When Presley suggested a Saturday morning walk with her sisters-in-law, I'd been a bit hesitant. These three spend so much time together, and even though I knew her first and she's my best friend, it's almost like Presley is closer with Lily and Penelope now. I don't like to feel like the odd one out and was anxious to try to converse with people who spoke to each other every day.

"Says the woman with three kids who looks like a supermodel daily." Lily rolls her eyes.

The baby whines for a moment, and Presley peaks inside, pulling back the blanket on her niece's body and rubbing her tummy a little. Lily smiles at Presley in thanks, and Molly is fast asleep before I can blink an eye.

"Jeez, who knew you were so good with kids," I say to Presley.

She shrugs. "Keaton and I babysit a lot for this growing brood."

"Speaking of growing, is there anything you want to tell us?" Penelope eyes her hopefully.

Presley shakes her long red locks. "Not yet, although we've been talking about starting to try."

That tidbit of information catches my attention. "Really? I thought you didn't know about kids."

We'd always talked about how neither of us was sure if we wanted to have children. Presley was too flighty, and I was too selfish. Listing off all the things I'd have to give up for a child ... it seemed endless. I wasn't sure if I wanted my life to change so drastically, and having a child meant putting everything you loved second.

Her green eyes are shifty as she glances from her sisters to me. "Well, I ... I know how great of a father Keaton would be. I feel like I'd be robbing him of fulfilling some destiny. And, well, babysitting has really given me the fever. If I get a baby half as good as Molly, I'll be lucky."

"I'll remember you said that when your little one is up at midnight, clawing at your boob," Penelope jokes.

Lily nods in agreement. "Although, it's the greatest thing on earth. I didn't know how badly I wanted to be a milk machine until I had a child."

I have to tamp down the shudder that runs through me because that doesn't sound at all like something I'd want.

The silence that follows when no one responds makes my skin crawl. Maybe they're not pushing the discussion further because I'm here, an intruder on their family talks.

"Ryan, I'm glad you're back in town. Are you working remotely?" Lily asks politely.

Penelope tunes in as Ames runs ahead of us, and Presley grins at me. They're all trying to make me feel included, which is nice, but I still feel like an outcast.

"I'm between projects right now."

It's a better line than, I'm taking a break from work. I feel like that would only worry people more, because my job has been my spouse for the last decade. But how do you explain that you feel you've ridden the roller coaster of a career to its end? Because that's how I feel. Once upon a time, I thought I had the sickest position in the game. Hacking or coding for whoever I wanted, wherever I wanted. Using the skills that came so easy to make massive amounts of money ... the kind I could never even have dreamed of as a kid.

But over the past two years, I've become resigned. My work doesn't bring me excitement anymore. Honestly, the last time I got any joy or spark from what I do was when Forrest asked me to consult on his cyber thief case.

So, I was taking some time off, until I could find something that inspired me again. I'd saved enough money, and I was staying for free with Presley and Keaton. Working my ass off for ten years ... yeah, I think I could afford to take a sabbatical.

"And you ... just came off a breakup, right?" Penelope's voice is cautious and delicate.

I assume Presley told them about my dating woes, if not an expanded version of the story. Everyone was probably wondering why I was here, anyway.

"Yep. It was pretty brutal. Found the bastard cheating on me, in our bed. With *two* women." That age-old practice of talking shit about men who've wronged us felt like an appropriate activity right now.

Plus, I hadn't gotten to vent much, and after rampaging

through my phone two days ago, deleting any evidence of him, it felt good to talk about.

"Oh, no he didn't! What a prick! Has he seen you? You're like Minka Kelly's younger, hotter sister." Penelope snaps her fingers as if she's about to fight Yanis on my behalf.

That makes me snort. "First off, Minka Kelly is already young and hot, way more so than me. Unfortunately, he had seen me, for a year and a half while we were in a relationship. The fucking Greek asshole. Claimed it was the European way."

"Language ..." Lily scolds me, eyes flicking to Molly and Ames.

I cover my mouth. "Whoops, sorry."

"Ignore her, my boys hear more cursing from their mother than they ever will on the school bus." Penelope rolls her eyes. "Anyway, I hope you slit his tires."

Shaking my head, I sigh. "I wish, but all he owns is a donkey and a moped. There was no need for a car where we lived. I did slap him in the face, though."

"Atta girl." Presley claps twice. "He deserves to fall all the way down those Santorini steps and right into the ocean."

"Oh, the bloody fantasies I've had about injuring him." My hands clasp together like I'm plotting his demise.

In truth, I could always feel something like that coming from Yanis. As much as I want to claim I was blindsided, I wasn't. He's a Greek artist, famous for being the next big thing in impressionist painting. From the moment I met him, I'd been swept up in his robust attitude for life, love, and good food. He gave me the grand tour of Greece, made me fall into bed with him, and I was fascinated ever since. But that little voice in the back of my head, and heart, told me there was something wrong. I knew I shouldn't have fully trusted him, and in the weeks leading up to his indiscretion, I'd already been thinking about how we were falling out of love. The spark wasn't there anymore, it had died out just like all the other affairs I'd sworn were epic love sagas and would never end.

This is how I was with men. I fell in love in two seconds, dove head first into a relationship and living together without a backward glance, and ended up royally fucking burned when it all came crashing down on top of my head.

"Well, Fawn Hill might be small, but there are a few eligible bachelors if you want us to set you up," Lily suggests cheerfully.

My fingers come up in a X. "No, thanks. I'm swearing off men for at least a year."

"Good for you." Penelope chuckles. "They're nothing but trouble, in all forms and ages. If I could trade mine all in for a week or two and sit in silence by myself, I would."

"Amen," Lily and Presley echo her.

I laugh because it's what I'm supposed to do, but I'm reminded by their sarcasm that they're all in loving, healthy relationships. Their husbands would all jump in front of a bullet for them, as opposed to lying and scamming.

And I know I claimed I wanted nothing to do with the single men of Fawn Hill, but I can't get the most enticing one out of my head.

It was only two days ago when Fletcher walked in on me butt naked and spilled all of his feelings about exploring my body. *Christ*, even thinking about it now makes my skin ignite and my stomach dip with temptation. The way I'd let his eyes comb over every inch of me for just a brief moment ... *Lord*, it had felt like I would combust from just his gaze alone. All the air had gone out of the room, and the sexual desire between us had practically suffocated me. It was dirty and yet *so* right.

For a brief second, I'd almost gone to him, asked for something that went completely against my vow to myself. By then Fletcher had done us both a favor and turned around, but not without obliterating me in the process.

"I've thought about this for a long time. Probably too often, if I'm being honest."

If he only knew …

"We'll beat them off with a stick, then. Anything for our girl." Presley slings an arm around my shoulder, trying to subtly hint that I was a part of their world now.

"Thanks. Hey, can we go get those sticky buns from the coffee shop? I've been dreaming about them since I left two years ago," I ask, trying to change the subject.

Penelope raises her hands, praising my suggestion. "Hell yes, I need sugar and carbs, stat."

Each plank of wood was smooth and soft to the touch, the work I've put in on each board apparent.

With a steady hand, I run the sander over the grain, rounding off any sharp edges or splinters. The pieces would have no hazards once they were stained and sealed, but you could never be too careful. This is the crib for my first niece, after all.

I hadn't known what to get Bowen and Lily when Molly was born and having little money to my name didn't help. But what I lacked in financial gains, I made up for in homemade gifts the past few years. First, it was the gift I gave Keaton and Presley for their wedding. Then, I built the flower arch that Bowen and Lily stood under for their wedding. Then I designed a bench for Bloomfield Park, and have done some other work for local friends and family.

Recently, I've been commissioned to design a chuppah for a prominent Jewish couple in New Jersey who found my work through Instagram. They surprised the hell of out of me when they offered two thousand dollars for the piece. It has been my largest sale thus far, and I've gotten a few inquiries recently just from their word-of-mouth praise.

I wasn't lying when I said I wanted to do this full time. Build furniture, make wooden art pieces, use my hands to distract from the shaking cravings that run through my body almost all hours of the day.

That's why I started doing this. At first, it had been model ships in rehab. One of my counselors there had suggested a distraction that got me off the grid of TV or Internet ... because alcohol commercials could pop up at any time. Even those were triggering for me back then. He said that reading could help, but my attention span was so shot that I gave up on that idea quickly. Arts and crafts were a last-ditch effort, that I found, shockingly, helpful.

I built three model ships during my time spent at the in-patient facility. Once I came home, I knew I had to find a way to distract myself from the constant temptation to drink.

It was fate that I stumbled on an old friend from high school who now ran his parent's farm. He'd randomly started talking about some scraps of woods and old pallets he needed help getting rid of. I offered to make use of them, take them off his hands ... and what started as just tinkering around with no knowledge or skill, turned into a passion.

Now, I can't imagine my life without it. Woodworking, turning scraps and discarded planks into something beautiful, there was a symmetry to it. A dedication that required time and great detail. When I finished a piece, I could gaze upon it with the utter satisfaction that my hands made that creation.

"That's looking great," I hear my twin brother's voice as I finish sanding off the last plank that will make up Molly's crib.

Turning, I spot Forrest standing in the doorway of the barn I use for my work. That friend I bumped into, Grady Burton, offered it to me when he saw what I did with the pallets. Call it a handout, but I took it willingly. The space is lofty enough that I didn't choke on sawdust, and out in the middle of several acres, so I could work in peace. In exchange, I help him out with whatever he needs, from hauling hay to harvesting crops.

"Yeah, I'm just trying to finish it. The kid will need a place of her own to sleep soon. Have you seen Bowen recently? He looks like an exhausted, caged tiger. The guy is going to keel over if he doesn't get some sleep and alone time with his wife soon."

Running a hand over the curved headboard piece of the crib, Forrest chuckles. "If he wanted alone time with his wife, he shouldn't have had a kid. Trust me, I know."

"Part of me still can't believe you're a family man." I wipe my sweaty forehead and grab the water jug off the folding table that doubles as a workbench, taking a large swig.

"Sometimes, I can't either. But, it's my life now. I wouldn't trade it for anything." He shrugs. "Hey, did you hear I caught another criminal? Just call me Detective Perfect Record."

And *there's* the twin I know. Forrest has always been the most boastful brother, probably because he feels the most unlike the rest of us. Where we were all blessed with baseball arms and charm, my lookalike got the wit and intellect. He's a damn genius, but I won't dare stroke his ego and tell him.

I applaud sarcastically. "We all live in a safer world simply because of you. All hail Forrest."

He rolls his eyes, knowing I'm mocking him. "By the way, did you steal my leather belt again? I can't find it anywhere."

Shit. I forgot I took that. "Maybe ..."

"Fletch, you know it's weird that you borrow clothes from your brothers, right?"

I shrug. "All the girls I know who have sisters do it. Your wife swaps wardrobes with Lily and Presley all the time."

"Because they're chicks. Guys don't do that," Forrest protests.

"Why can't we? I don't feel like going to the store to grab a new belt, and I know you have a couple. It saves us all money. I'll let you borrow something of mine so we can call it even."

My brother shakes his head. "That logic doesn't make sense. Would you let Bowen borrow your boxers?"

I consider this. "If he needed them."

"So, you'd wear a piece of clothing that your brother's ball sweat was on?" Forrest's mouth is set in a deep frown, and he cringes from the idea.

Placing the water jug, half empty now, back on my makeshift workbench, I pick up a can of stain and a paintbrush.

"I mean, I guess if I didn't have another option. Or if they had a cool print. Like big fluffy dogs or something. Or maybe rocket ships. Boxers have to have a cool print, or you don't have that secret, confident swag under your clothes."

Forrest ponders my last sentence. "Hmm, I guess you might be right. I do have some sick plaid briefs that Penelope loves ..."

I begin slathering stain onto the smooth planks that will assemble to make the crib.

"You need something? You know why I work all the way out here ..." My family knows my preference for being alone while I'm creating.

He walks over to the other side of the barn, inspecting some of the half-finished stuff I've cast aside for the crib project.

"What's this going to be?" he asks, his hands pulling out a large, circular object.

I glance over my shoulder, starting to get annoyed by his presence. "A clock. I'm trying to teach myself about how to build one using all wooden gears, hands, inner-workings, that sort of thing."

My brother studies it. "You'll have to put the gears like this."

He makes a motion with his hands, and of course, it took him less than three seconds to figure out how to build one when I've been reading books on it for three weeks.

"Do you need something?" I snap, wanting him gone.

I only have so much time to come out here and work between my shifts at the grocery store, helping Grady, helping Mom, babysitting, and all the other shit that takes me away from my passion.

"Saw Ryan walking home from the yoga studio the other day." Forrest drops this casually into conversation like I don't know what he's trying to get at.

"You're my twin brother. We have the same mind. Yes, I know she's in town. No, I don't want to talk about it. No, I'm not going to stand here and gossip about chicks with you while you, the married man, tries to set me up."

"There has always been that thing between you," he points out, still trying to badger me about this.

"Forrest, drop it. I'm not dating, you know that. And the first time I met Ryan, everyone was trying to fix *you two* up."

He waves this off like he didn't have her staying with him the last time I saw her two years ago. "That's ancient history, and we had zero chemistry. I'm a happily married man, now. Who just wants to see his baby brother happy."

I roll my eyes. "You're older by half a minute."

"Thirty-seven seconds to be exact." he counters.

"Whatever. Regardless, I don't want to be with anyone. I'm focusing on me and am in no place to take care of someone else."

Forrest comes to sit and watch me work, taking up the empty stool next to my folding table.

"Fletch, it's been almost five years. Don't they tell recovering alcoholics not to get into a relationship for the first year? You've held up that promise four times over. And your promise to yourself was that you'd never be involved with a woman again until it was the real deal. Brother, I'm telling you that you and Ryan could be the real deal. Everyone sees it, we all feel those fuck me vibes whenever you two are in the same room. Hell, when she came to help me with that case, I thought you two were going to bone on the couch in front of me."

I try to ignore the blaring facts alarm going off in my head because it too remembers how much I jerked off to fantasies of Ryan in the weeks after I'd found her at Forrest's old place. But his tone is pissing me off, as is his message.

"Will everyone just get off my dick about this? Jesus, the woman hasn't been in town more than a week and I've seen the way everyone is frothing at the mouth for us to fall madly in love."

He holds his hands up in surrender. "All right, all right. I'm just looking out for you. When you decide to get off your celibate soapbox and apply logic to your life, call me."

With that, Forrest hops off the stool and exits my barn, leaving me to work in peace.

But damn him, I can't stop hearing the echo of his words in my ears.

The jerk planted this seed of an idea, that Ryan could be the girl I could get serious about, and it won't stop pressing at my frontal lobe.

I'm going to have to pummel him for this.

"You're seriously allowing your kid to have a manhunt party for his birthday?"

I look skeptically at Penelope, my sister-in-law. She married my twin brother, Forrest, two years ago in a courthouse ceremony. And my brother then adopted her three young boys. Surprisingly, he's become one of the best father figures I've ever witnessed interact with children. Who would have known? I was happy for him though and having three rowdy nephews keeps me on my toes.

"Take that judgment out of your tone, Fletcher," Penelope scolds me, setting up a table in their driveway.

She throws a colorful tablecloth over the folding table and then begins putting cups, plates and plastic silverware on top. It's dusk, with the summer sun sending rays cascading over the rooftops of the houses in her and Forrest's neighborhood.

"I'm just saying ... it's a game where people hunt other people in the dark and then drag them back to the 'jail.' Which in this case, is your garage. You don't think this could get ugly? Or some other mischief could be happening out in those woods?" I raise an eyebrow, trying to suggest something.

"He's twelve, Fletcher. If you don't think any of those boys or girls in his grade haven't kissed each other yet, I don't want to know how oblivious you'll be as a parent."

Forrest snorts at his wife's tongue lashing of me. "And when did you become so morally righteous? What were you doing as a twelve-year-old?"

Well, maybe he has a point. I was stealing cans of beer from Keaton and Bowen's parties in the farm fields. And actually, probably doing much worse than an innocent game of manhunt.

"Fine, if this is what the kid wants for his birthday, I'll make it the best damn manhunt party he's ever seen." I clap my hands together.

"Uncle Fletch! Uncle Fletch!" Matthew and Travis run into the driveway, the garage lights from several houses illuminating the block.

"My dudes!" I high five my adopted nephews and then ruffle their hair.

Who knew I'd love being an uncle so much? The kids are a blast, and I get to let my goofy side out, even more, when I'm with them. I help Forrest and Penelope out a lot by picking them up from practice or school, and they look at me as more of a friend than an authority figure. I know that Molly will do the same one day, but for now, she just has me wrapped around her miniature-sized pinky.

"Are you going to be on my team?" Travis bounces up and down, not yet at the age where excitement is no longer cool.

"You bet your ass I am." I elbow him after I curse, and the boys giggle. "We're going to crush those hiders. How many kids you got coming to this thing, anyway?"

He ponders the question for a minute, while Matthew begins sneaking bites of cookie off the snack table his mom set up. "About thirty. Plus all the old people."

And by old people, he means my brothers, sisters-in-law, and myself. Damn, are we really being called the oldies now?

"Well, the old people might just kick your butt." Bowen comes walking up, hand in hand with Lily.

They greet me with a fist bump and a hug respectively. "Where is baby lady tonight?"

Lily's eyes look weepy. "Eliza is watching her, she's already asleep. I'll have to run home in a few hours to feed her, but Bowen thought it would be fun to get out."

"Don't sound so miserable about it." Bowen kisses his wife's forehead as she sniffles. "Molly is fine, babe, and it'll be fun to get out just the two of us for a little while."

"You're right. I just miss her already." My sister-in-law blinks rapidly, and Bowen leads her away for some privacy.

"Okayyyy," I blow out a breath, not wanting to deal with that kind of emotional baggage tonight. "Let's get this party started!"

About half an hour later, nightfall has descended, and so have the town's pre-teens. They're all gathered in the driveway, listening to Penelope lay ground rules about the game.

"You're going to split into two teams, one will hide first and the others will hunt. No straying, if we get a call that you're on Main Street, you've gone too far. No physical violence, we're not playing tackle and capture here. If I find you destroying property, I'll escort you down to the police station myself. Don't spook the neighbors, who have been warned about this little game going on. All in all, have fun, but be respectful!"

I'd say that's a fair ask, and the kids don't voice any objections. I can see a couple of the boys and girls eyeing each other, and it makes me nostalgic. I remember the days of first crushes and innocent flirting.

"Okay, split up, and we'll give the hiders a five-minute head start. Go!" Forrest yells, and all the kid's scatter.

"I'm going to own these kids!" I holler, feeling the adrenaline course through me.

So, what, I'm almost thirty and still enthused by backyard games? I've used about eight of my nine lives and have to find enjoyment in the little things.

The world goes silent as some hide and others try to sneak up on them, and I edge around the side of Forrest's house. My feet tread lightly, and a summer breeze brushes through my T-shirt as I snoop about.

There is a form in the shadows, and I smirk at how poorly someone hid. Here, in the trees behind Penelope and Forrest's house, is such an obvious hiding spot. Or maybe that's what they were going for, thinking that no one would check here because everyone would run miles away.

I skirt around the other side of the clump of hedges, careful not to make too much noise or the person will suspect me and flee. When I'm close enough, I reach out a hand, grab them by the upper arm, and whisper, "Gotcha."

"Oh my God!" A female voice yelps, and from the sound, I know she's not Travis' age.

She moves into the light a bit, the moon illuminating one side of her face.

"Ryan?" My heart rate kicks up as I realize I've come across the one person I never thought I'd be hunting.

"Fletcher ... jeez, you scared the crap out of me." Five black-painted fingernails come up to massage her chest, like she's recovering from a mild shock.

"I didn't realize you were playing. I didn't see you in the driveway." I'm dumbfounded, and acutely aware that we're alone, secluded in the bushes.

"I was standing out back with Keaton and Presley when Forrest yelled to start hiding. So, I made a dash for it. Figured, why not partake in the fun?"

She had the same idea I did. "Right."

The silence envelops us, and we should move out of the hiding spot, but neither of us moves. An enchanting magnetism draws us closer, and rather than announce that I've captured a prisoner, I stay quiet, staring at her as she stares at me.

I shouldn't do this, admire her fox-like features or search for answers to questions I can't ask in those whiskey-colored eyes. My hand hasn't moved from where it lightly holds her arm, and the longer I keep it there, the bigger the hole I'm digging myself into.

But, it could just be something we leave out here in the dark. A stolen moment between us that only the night will witness and won't leave us tied to anything.

Without thinking further, my free hand reaches up to catch the silky ends of her locks, the dark hair slipping through my fingers like smooth silk. Ryan's eyes flick down to where I touch her, and her eyes flutter closed as if I've put my hands in the most intimate of places. My God, is she sexy ... and we're both fully clothed, having only the lightest of contact.

"Fletcher ..." The way she says my name is different than anyone who has ever called me by it before.

"Hm?" I ask distractedly, my gaze catching on her lips as she speaks.

Full and transfixing, I know that in the daylight they're the color of ripe plums. I study them as they move again.

"Are you going to kiss me?" Ryan breathes, and my eyes flick up to hers.

The expression in them isn't rejecting, but it isn't inviting either. She's not asking me *to* kiss her, she's asking if I'm *going* to. I'm not sure what's worse; being asked to kiss her when I know it will only harm both of us in the long run, or not knowing if she wants me to when I've decided it's the only thing I want on earth.

The brush of her fingers over my tricep sends goose bumps over my flesh, and I realize she's just touched me, too. Our mouths are inches apart now, and whether or not either of us have mentally agreed to this kiss, it seems to be happening.

Her scent catches in my nostrils, feminine and somewhat overpowering, in the best way possible. But it's her perfume that finally breaks the spell, instead of spurring me to run faster in the direction of danger.

"No," I answer her question, untangling my fingers from her strands and backing away.

Because once I taste her, I know it will never be enough. I've barely been alone with her, but I feel it deep in my bones. There is something addicting about Ryan Shea. Which is the worst possible thing for me.

She eyes me warily, but almost in an understanding way, as I retreat backward, our eyes never dropping from one another.

I nod, hoping she gets why I can't kiss her. On some deeper level, I feel more connected to this woman than almost anyone else in my life, and I don't even know why.

Ryan nods back, confirming that she sees who I am past the face I put on for most people.

The chiming of my ringtone wakes me from a dreamless sleep, panic hitting me as I sit up in bed.

No matter why your phone goes off at three a.m., it's always going to incite some kind of fear. I throw the rumpled sheets off my body, disoriented in the strange guest cottage in the pitch-black night.

What if something was really wrong with Presley? No, they would have come out to tell me if that was it.

If this was Yanis blowing up my phone in the middle of the night, I was going to fucking kill him. Or better yet, block him entirely from ever calling me again. Which I should have already done, I know.

My hands fumble around in the dark, trying to grab at my phone which is still vibrating on some surface. Finally, I find it, and pick it up while squinting against the bright screen.

"Hello?" I say groggily, pushing a few sweaty strands from my face.

"Ryan? You picked up! Aw, listen, girl, I really need you. I got some people on my ass, and there is just some money ..."

My blood goes cold in my veins, that sinking feeling of dread dropping my stomach down to my toes. Fuck, I hadn't thought of the possibility of *her* calling.

Natasha rambles on in the background, while I try to keep my composure. I don't call my mother by anything but her first name, simply because she gave me up when I was three years old and drifted in and out of my life for years until I put a stop to it.

"I'm not sending you any more money." I put my foot down, stopping her drug-fueled diatribe.

I've learned that mistake the hard way, many times. It started when I was fifteen and would send her any bit of my after-school job pay. And then when I was twenty, in college, and would shave off portions of my scholarship-awarded stipends. Then again, at twenty-four, when I was earning good money with my first company. Each time, I believed she'd use the money to get clean, to go to rehab and come back into my life as a real parent.

The last time I sent her funds, she'd nearly overdosed and I got the call from the hospital as her emergency contact. When I'd gone to visit her in the room she was admitted to, I barely recognized her. Her skin was gray, her hair missing in patches, and so many track marks up her arm, it looked like an angry cat had gone to town on it. I was so disgusted, I puked in the adjoining hospital room bathroom.

I didn't have the heart to completely block her number, call me an idiot, I know.

"Aw, come on, sweetheart. Don't you want to help out your dear old mama?" Her voice was scratchy, as if she'd smoked every pack of cigarettes in America.

Considering she'd given me up at birth, put me into some of the worst foster homes imaginable, and didn't give a real shit about me, was it any wonder I didn't want to help her fuel her heroin habit? But I don't say that, it's no use. I've tried to have that logical discussion before, and it only ended with me in tears and her immature, destroyed brain confused over why I would have any problem with her.

"I'm not sending you anything. Don't call here again, Natasha." My stomach is in knots, because there is a very good chance I could never talk to her again.

Why did I still care for this useless piece of a human? Because she was my biological mother, and we were all apparently born with unconditional love for them ... no matter how horribly they treat us.

"You know, you're some high and mighty bitch, you little—"

I cut her off before she can hurl more insults at me, clicking the red button on the screen to hang up abruptly.

"Fuck," I mutter, running my hands through my disheveled hair.

I'll never be able to sleep after that rousing conversation. My legs shake unconsciously on the bed, and I huff a frustrated breath as I stand and walk out of the guest cottage. Outside, the night is muggy and does nothing to relieve the pent-up anger in my chest.

Crossing the backyard, I gently and quietly slide open the door to the kitchen, silently thanking Presley for keeping it open in case I need a midnight cereal binge. Right now, though, I need something stronger than cereal.

Breaking open the bar cart that Keaton keeps on the other side of their island, I select a single malt scotch and pour a heavy hand into a highball glass. The first sip numbs my jumpy limbs, and the second and third start to drown my anxious thoughts.

"Someone else needs a nightcap, I see."

Hattie, Presley's grandmother, walks into the kitchen. I rush to her, hugging her tightly.

"I didn't realize you were staying here tonight!" I keep my excited voice quiet.

"A pipe burst in my bathroom and soaked the whole bedroom carpet. I'll be staying a day or two while it gets fixed. Apologies for not visiting sooner, you know I adore you, girl."

The warm smile that stretches my lips is genuine. "And I adore you. Can I pour you a glass? What's keeping you up?"

She grunts as she takes a seat at the kitchen table, and I start fixing her a drink. "At my age, you don't sleep much anymore. Just catnaps here and there. But my old bones are too stiff and pained to lie down flat in a bed for long. And what, might I ask, woke you up?"

Bringing both our drinks, I sit next to her at the table. "A phone call."

We both sip, the bitter liquor burning as it slides down my throat.

"Who was on the other end? Not that prick, I hope."

Of course, Presley told Hattie. Her grandmother has a way of pulling information out of anyone with a pulse. I don't mind though, Hattie only wants the best for me, and I know it.

"No, thank God. I'm done wasting time on his excuses, or him in general."

She pats my knee. "Good to hear. So, who woke you?"

I take a large gulp before I answer. "My mother."

"Ah." Hattie sips, ruminating. "You know, you don't have to waste time on her excuses, either."

"I know that. But with her, it's not that simple." My fingers tap the side of the glass.

"No, I suppose it's not," she agrees.

We drink in silence for a few minutes, and then Hattie speaks again.

"Ryan, you have had a tough life. I'm not sure anyone in this town, or anyone you consider a friend, really grasps how much shit you've had to shovel. Being abandoned, as a child, it does a number on you … one I don't fully grasp because I haven't walked in your shoes. And I know why you turn to men to fill that love tank of yours, why you think their approval and affection will make it full. I'm also aware that you know you're a strong, capable woman … one who can kick ass in the boardroom or the bedroom. But something, deep down in that closed off heart of yours, is broken. You think you give these men love, but you've never truly gifted your heart to anyone. Because the first person who was supposed to take care of it, completely broke it. Over and over again, I'm sure your mother lets you down. I'm an old woman, so I can say these things without having explicit knowledge on the specific subject. So, I'm going to tell you that, until you cut out the cancer that is your mother, you will never truly be able to be with someone as a whole person."

Hattie's words are harsh, and tears prick at the corners of my eyes. Maybe it's the whiskey, because I'm not usually a crier, or maybe it's that she's so brutally correct.

But she's wrong, in a way. Someone in this town does know me … sees inside my soul and understands on a deeper level than he should be able to.

When Fletcher found me during the manhunt game earlier tonight, it had been fate meddling again. What were the chances? First, the drive into town, and then him walking into my guest cottage. The third time, and it was more than just a coincidence now. I am a science girl through and through, but the universe is clearly sending me signals and I am not against believing in superstition if it's trying to tell me something.

And when he hunted me down, not on purpose, I could feel the tension between us coming to a tee. That's why I'd asked if he was going to kiss me. Because my promise to myself was to stay away from men, but Fletcher seemed to be digging himself into my thoughts like a stubborn splinter. If he is going to go for it, I am not going to stop him.

Though, Fletcher seemed to stop on both our behalves. It's as if he knew my moral dilemma and had an almost identical one. We could act on this, and maybe it would be great. But, more likely, we would only end up in worse condition than we are right now. I appreciate his ability to act rationally.

Still, I would love to know what it would feel like to kiss him.

Hattie stands. "I'm headed back up for a cat nap before dawn. Come find me tomorrow, I could use your help with something."

Her complete redirection throws me off, leaving the advice she'd just shot me straight with echoing around in my brain.

"What's that?" I finish off my glass and clear both to the sink.

"There is an advanced computer course at the middle school during the summer months, but the teacher is an incompetent moron. I volunteer about town, since I sold the shop, and someone in the receptionist's office mentioned that the kids needed to learn coding. I think you'd be perfect to help them."

"Aw, Hattie, I don't know—" I start to object, because I'm not a kid person, nor do I have the patience to teach.

"Hush, child. No one says no to me. It would serve you good to just shut up and show up when you're told. It's not like you're busy with anything else, hiding out here. I'll see you tomorrow."

Keeping my mouth shut, I nod, because what else am I going to do.

When I finally do stumble back to the cottage, more tipsy for the wear, I collapse onto the bed and fall into another dark, dreamless sleep.

FLETCHER

Examining my online bank account, I tilt my head.

In a good way, that is. Because I've saved way more than I previously thought. It's almost like digging in your pockets and finding a twenty-dollar bill. Except, in this case, I found thousands more than I thought.

Shit, I've been way more frugal than I thought I'd been. Which means ... I can finally attempt to do something I've been waiting years to do.

Shutting my laptop, I throw on a pair of sneakers and a ball cap. Mom is already dozing in her rocker in the living room, Alex Trebek asking questions on the TV. Planting a kiss on her forehead, I quietly leave the house.

Opting to walk the mile over to Forrest and Penelope's place, I turn my face upward to the setting sun. Summer is my favorite season in Fawn Hill. Being outside does something good for my soul, I'm far too jumpy being cooped up in the winter. Plus, I'm not freezing my nuts off while I walk across town.

My mind strays to Ryan, and what she's doing over at Presley and Keaton's house. Poker night isn't there, and as much as I've denied myself when it comes to her, part of me kind of wishes I was seeing her tonight.

Is she thinking about our almost kiss? How long is she staying in town?

I haven't seen her in a week, since that night. I've been busy in the wood shop, and at work. And she is busy with ... well, I'm not sure. I can't exactly ask about her daily activities or how long her stay will be, because then my family will only meddle harder.

I arrive at Forrest's and realize that I'm the last one to the party. Bowen and Keaton's cars are here, and when I walk in the side door without bothering to knock, I don't hear the kids.

"Are the kids asleep?" I ask Penelope when I find her in the kitchen, pouring herself a glass of red.

She kisses me on the cheek and picks up her wine. "Nope, they're at Marion's for the night. You guys are having poker night, and Mama is watching *The Bachelor* with a drink."

My eyes avoid looking at the bottle, but I can still smell it and I back away toward the door to the basement. "Sounds great, have fun."

It's been five years, and still, my fingers ache to reach out and grasp that bottle in my hands.

"Hey, man. What took you so long?" Keaton asks when I step off the last stair.

Forrest and Penelope finished their basement about six months ago. It's a full-on separate apartment almost, with a tiny kitchen, a pullout couch, a bathroom with a shower stall and vintage arcade games for the boys. I would have considered moving in here, if they'd asked and I was able to put up with the chaos of their household on a daily basis. Which I was not.

My brothers have cleaned out the downstairs bar and taking the place of Bowen's favorite bottles are liters of soda, iced tea, and lemonade. I appreciate that they keep poker night a sober event for me, hell, it's probably bad enough I'm gambling. But card games were never my problem and aren't the things that trigger me to want to drink.

Everything triggers me to want to drink, on a minute-by-minute basis. I figure I shouldn't have to rule out guy time with my brothers just because I crave the smooth burn of bourbon sliding down my throat every second.

"I walked here," I say, grabbing an iced tea and joining them.

Bowen shuffles the deck and deals. "Get ready to give me your money, suckers."

"Nah, I'm feeling lucky tonight. Plus, my roof." Forrest points up.

I just smirk, because I'm usually the victor here. My brothers have lousy poker faces, especially Keaton.

"I'm not even going to attempt to brag, because we all know I'm crap," my oldest brother admits.

"That's his one curse word for the week and we got to witness it!" Forrest teases.

Glancing down at my first hand, I ask for two new cards in exchange for the ones I discard. My brother's heads are buried in their own hands, but by the crease in Bowen's brow, and the way Keaton is chewing his lip, I know I can manage to pick up a better combination of cards than them. Forrest is a little tougher, especially because my twin and I usually play very similarly.

"Hey, do you guys know of any cheap listings in town?" I throw the question out, knowing they're going to start prying.

But since looking at my bank account, it's all I can think about.

"You mean house listings?" Bowen asks, curious.

"Yeah. I've checked into my finances, and I think I'm ready."

"To buy something? You sure you want that much responsibility?" Keaton eyes me.

And here we go. "Yes, *Dad*. I'm almost thirty fucking years old and live in Mom's guest room, believe me, I think I know how to handle myself."

All three of my brothers exchange a look, and suddenly I'm envisioning slitting their throats with my cards.

"What?" I cry, exasperated.

My twin speaks up. "It's just ... you don't want a house. It's so much work, and if I had to do it again as a bachelor, I totally would have rented a small place. It was dumb to own a whole home, and I didn't use half of it."

"What you're saying is, you all think it's a bad idea for me to get my own place. Just admit it, I'm not a moron, despite your opinions of me."

I was only saying what everyone in the room was thinking. I'm not sure why my temper is getting the best of me ... honestly, most of the time, I'm a really laid-back guy. Probably because, for the past five years, I've proven to myself and everyone around me that I can be sober, responsible, reliable, and all the other positive personality attributes you can think of. I've spent a lot of time repenting and allowing my family to keep me under close watch.

And now, the first time I try to tell them I'm ready to spread my wings, they're batting me back down to the ground.

Keaton's face frowns in sympathy, and I know what he's about to say is all going to be pandering bullshit.

"That's not what we're saying, Fletch. We're just ... we worry about you. We see how well you're doing, and how great your life is right now, and we just want the best for you. You're doing good at Mom's, with your job and your woodworking ... why change something? Consistency is best, correct? Buying a home, it's a big step with lots of frustrations and problems that could arise. You don't need that kind of stress."

I want to throttle him, and I have to bite the back of my tongue *hard* to keep from letting my fury out. They all look at me like the little brother slash screw-up that they still think I am. Have I ever interfered in their lives, or kicked them while they were down? Not once. Yet, they always seem to be ready and willing to do it to me.

"Have you not been watching for the last five years while I clean my life up and get it in working order? Do I not show up for Mom more than any of you these days? Have I found a passion that I'm good at, that I have begun to make money off of? When will my recovery be enough for you guys to look at me like a normal person, instead of your alcoholic, troublemaker brother?"

And that's the crux of it. What has been weighing on me for so long, just knocking at my heart to be let out. They don't view me on the same level as themselves, and that's why this is working me up so much.

I throw my cards down, more than done with this poker night. Fuck, I need a meeting so bad right now.

Without another word to my brothers, I march up the stairs and out of Forrest's house. Their calls after me hit my ears, but I don't stop.

I fume down the street, speed-walking away from the house toward Mom's. It's nearly nine o'clock, which means I won't be able to get to an AA meeting until tomorrow morning. My throat is dry and my fingertips are cold, and this is the time I know I'm most vulnerable. When nothing I can think of in the world sounds like it will make me feel better.

That's when alcohol, my old buddy, pops into my head. Alcohol always made me feel better. It picked me up when I felt worthless. It wrapped a warm arm around me when the girl I wanted went home with someone else. It kept me company when everyone else was moving on with their lives.

Fuck. Fuck, fuck, *fuck*.

I'm jonesing, and I know it. So I pull out my cell phone, tapping on the first number on my favorites screen.

"Fletch, how's your night?"

Cookie's warm, raspy voice fills my ear, and instantly, I can feel my anxiety level lower.

"Not great." I blow out a breath of air, stopping as I turn the corner onto an unlit street.

I take a seat on the curb and rest my elbows on my knees, almost needing to take a pause and regroup.

"Tell me about it," my sponsor says, knowing that I both need a moment, but need to vent.

The first time I went to an AA meeting, after I left rehab, I was so freaked out; I didn't talk the entire time. I sat there listening to stories of people who were twenty years sober, of others who had stolen money from their family or gotten so drunk that they'd ended up face down in a pond, gasping for air when their nervous system finally woke them up. One guy had smashed into a family of five on their way home from church, injuring all and almost killing one of them. He'd gone to prison for seven years and had been sober for fifteen.

What struck me most about the meeting though, was how not alone I felt. I'd never, in my life, encountered people who spoke about alcohol the way I thought about it. Like it was inevitable to consume, an old lover whom you both hated and desperately needed. For years, I thought my relationship with drinking was just more severe than those of my imbibing, partying counterparts.

Being in that meeting had shown me, truly, that I had a problem ... but I wasn't the only one.

Cookie had approached me when I'd shown up for the third time and asked if I had a sponsor yet. I remember thinking that forty years ago, she was probably a knockout. With dark brown hair, that she still dyes well into her mid-sixties, a full face of makeup, bangle bracelets up her arms and a love for recalling her Woodstock days ... I was instantly drawn to her. The quiet calm she had, paired with a no-nonsense attitude, was exactly what I needed in a sponsor.

We've been meeting once a week, every week, for four-and-a-half years.

I run my free hand through my hair, exasperated but relieved that she's here to listen. "It's my brothers, again. We had poker night tonight, and I asked them if they knew of any home listings in town that were cheap. Like you and I have talked about, I think it might be time for me to move out on my own. Of course, they just started shooting holes in the plan before they even listened to what I was saying. Said a house was a lot of upkeep, that I didn't want to deal with that shit ... but I knew they were just doing that polite thing people do when they want to talk you out of something. It pisses me off that they don't have my back."

"Why does it piss you off?" Cookie asks, and I know she's playing the therapist part of the sponsor role.

"Because I've worked really fucking hard to get to where I am. I feel like I've proven myself in the past couple of years, and I've done it all while maintaining my sobriety. When is it going to be enough for them to forget about the mistakes I've made?"

Cookie sighs on the other end, and I know she's probably sitting in her screened-in porch, smoking a cigarette.

"Kid, most people never forget the mistakes of others. And for your family, as well as the people I wronged when I was drinking myself to death ... a big part of their memory when it comes to you is pulling you out of that meth house and driving you to rehab. It's just a fact, sweetheart. A crap one that all alcoholics have to come to terms with. The people you hurt may forgive you, they may love you, but we don't have a stun gun or something that can erase your worst moments in their heads."

I nod, not that she can see it. It's one of the hardest things I've had to come to grips with in the recovery process. I know I fucked up, I know my brothers know that, and I know they have every right to be skeptical of my every move. But ... I just wish it didn't have to be that way.

"Do you think moving out is a bad idea?" My voice is anxious, because her opinion matters to me.

Cookie knows who I am, maybe more than a lot of people close to me. Because we share the same demon.

"Doll, I have a favor I can call in. I personally think it'd be good for you to get out of your mama's house. Now, I agree with your brothers; owning a house is a pain in the ass and not something you ought to do right now. But, I do think you're ready for a space of your own. Let me see what I can wrangle up, and I'll let you know by the end of next week."

A breath of relief whooshes out. Just talking to her makes the knot between my shoulders ease.

"Thanks, Cookie."

"Now, let me sleep. I'm an old woman, and if this isn't a booty call, talking to anyone this late isn't worth losing beauty rest."

Chuckling, I bid her good night and then walk the rest of the way home.

"And, that's how you build a simple website using the most basic form of HTML."

I finish my lecture, glancing around the room at the kid's computer screens. The class is comprised of six girls and four boys, and I'm geeky enough to admit that I'm fucking pumped this summer STEM class has girls as its majority gender.

The afternoon hasn't been as bad as I thought it would be. Actually, it was kind of fun. I went all the way back to the basics, starting at the simplest level for these middle schoolers who were blank slates when it came to anything hacking or coding.

Ten faces stare back at me, expressions ranging from satisfied with themselves to anxious with more questions they want to ask me. I've never felt this sense of contentment, of going through an entire lesson and imparting knowledge to someone else. Not even when I've coded a huge project or found where a data leak came from when a Fortune 500 hundred company hires me.

"Ryan, how would I add a scrolling header? Say, if I wanted

to add more than one picture or add to the top of the website?" Marie, a girl in a Slytherin shirt with beautiful dark curls, asks.

I click back onto my display screen, splashed across the whiteboard from a projector in the ceiling, to show them how I do it on my own desktop. I can hear a few of them clicking around, and others just watching me.

I forgot what it was like, to discover the great wide world of the Internet ... and its underworld. When I first started dabbling in coding and hacking, I'd just been playing around by myself. I was a self-taught woman; sure, college courses helped refine my skills, but by the time I went to my alma mater, I was surfing around the dark web with Internet dregs ten years my senior.

Watching these kids' brains open up to the possibilities of what a computer held, and what it could do at their disposal ... it was the first real moment of passionate interest I've had for my craft in a long time.

"I think that went well." Hattie nods as the bell rings to end the period, pleased with me and probably herself for suggesting it.

"Me too, and I have to say ... it was kind of fun." A small smile graces my lips as I watch the kids rush off to their next class.

She claps me on the back. "Good, we'll see you next week then."

"Wait ... what?" I scramble, trying to find an excuse about why I can't come back to teach.

"You're sticking around for the foreseeable future, am I right? I don't imagine you've found the answers to your internal dilemma just yet. So in the meantime, you can come here once a week and teach these kids. Because they enjoy it, and I think you do, too."

Now I see why Presley always says she loves Hattie, but she's pushy as hell. She is right, though ... I don't have much going on.

And I still feel lost in my life, as if I'm searching for something. Teaching these kids once a week until I find what my next adventure might be, well, it could be fun.

"All right. I'll see you next week. Or at home, in the middle of the night for a midnight drink." I wink at her and see myself out, walking through the halls of the middle school.

This might not be my middle school, but it takes me back. The lockers, the smell of teenage angst and body odor in the air. Even in the summer, the bell system is still active, and the chime of it takes me back. I'm in a nostalgia-filled bubble by the time I reach the front of the school, pushing through the doors.

I peel the visitor sticker off my shirt, crumple it, and throw it in one of the garbage cans near the front pillar. Without a car, I can't go anywhere far, so it's a good thing Fawn Hill Middle School is only a stone's throw from its measly Main Street. Plus, I'm a New Yorker ... I'm used to hoofing it in heels for sixteen blocks.

An afternoon coffee, preferably iced with a pump of vanilla syrup, sounds like the perfect treat. The July sun is scorching, but I'm kind of getting used to the blinding heat of a small-town summer. In the city, the sun falls behind skyscrapers, and it's all sweaty subway cars and rankled men in black business suits.

But here, out in the country, the air smells so sweet in the sunshine that I can practically inhale the rolling hills past Main Street. Everywhere you go, you're met with harsh rays that lick up your skin, but the vitamin D leaves such a pleasant feeling that it's easy to mind the humidity.

I'm almost at the coffee shop, my mouth watering for that cold brew, when my path is interrupted.

Up the sidewalk, a bunch of people suddenly emerge from the entrance of what looks like a church. I watch them, men and women, shuffle out, some of their faces neutral while others looked deep in thought.

Suddenly, the crowd parts and I see Fletcher, his hands stuffed in his pockets as he walks right toward me.

I contemplate ducking behind a garbage can in front of me, but then decide that is not at all something I would do. I am not a coward, even if the man makes my heartbeat jump into my throat every time I see him. Though as I near the church, and come so close to contact with Fletcher, I see the sign announcing why all of those people had been in there.

Alcoholics Anonymous.

The bottom of my stomach clenches, low and nauseous, and a barrage of emotions come over me. Fletcher was just in there, at an AA meeting. He's an addict, just like ...

My mother.

I remember now, Presley mentioning something about this before, but I'd honestly forgotten. And it all comes rushing back; how he didn't drink at their wedding, or accompany us out to the Goat & Barrister, the local Fawn Hill bar, whenever I was in town.

"Uh, hi," I say awkwardly, Fletcher approaching before I can carefully rearrange my expression to not look judgy or surprised.

He holds up his hand in a brisk wave, and then shoves it down in his pockets, looking like a man caught red-handed. "Hey. Uh ..."

We both just kind of stand there, the uncomfortableness growing by the second.

"I was just in a meeting." He points back toward the church, because this is so weird that we can't not acknowledge it.

I shake my head, waving him off. "That's supposed to be anonymous, right? You don't need to explain."

"Ryan, you just saw me walk out of there. I'm not ashamed of it, and it would be fucking strange if I tried to lie about it." He chuckles, and I swallow watching the Adam's apple bob under the tanned skin of his throat.

And just like that, he manages to erase most of the comparisons between my mother and him I'd been making in my head. Fletcher is standing in front of me, sober and honest. He's not shrinking away from me, making excuses or acting defensively to save his own ass. I may not know him well, but I think I'm a pretty good judge of character, and I know when someone is lying to me. My entire relationship with my mother has been her sneaking around, acting suspicious, and breaking my heart around every corner.

In one encounter, Fletcher has owned up to his shortcomings, and laid them right out in the open between us.

"I'm glad you're getting the help you need." I nod, not sure how to proceed.

Fletcher's sea-blue eyes study my face, and the warmth of the small smile turning his mouth up at the corners has me wanting to move in closer.

"Can I buy you a coffee?" he asks as if reading my mind.

And even though I know I shouldn't open this can of worms, my brain rejects everything else but the word *yes*.

11

I set the large vanilla iced coffee down in front of Ryan and then place my medium cold brew across from it.

Before I take the empty seat on the other side of the table, I grab the apple turnover and two forks I left waiting on the counter.

"You didn't have to buy this. I could have gotten mine," she protests half-heartedly after the fact.

"Don't worry about it. The owner owes me a favor." I toss a nod to Carlton, the coffee shop owner who I've known ... well, probably my entire life.

"Still, you didn't have to. And a sweet treat? It's too much." Her smile is sarcastic, and my heart goes to shit.

Beating all wild and crazy, that I have to stamp out its hope and frivolity with a pointer finger to the chest. As if I'm telling my own organ to knock it off.

I hand her a fork and don't wait before I dig into my half of the apple turnover. The sweetness and tartness explode in my mouth, and I sigh at the much-needed dessert after the dreaded AA meeting. It's not that I don't want to go to meetings, hell, I know it's vital for my recovery and continued sobriety.

But something about being in that basement made me feel like I was being slowly strangled. Especially when listening to newly sober peers, those with a one day chip, or someone who fell off the wagon and had to start fresh. We had one of those today, a guy who'd chucked his thirteen-year recovery out the window for a bottle of Jack on a day he was feeling particularly low. Watching him stand at the podium and tearfully fight his way through his new reality was soul-crushing.

We eat in silence for a moment, sipping our coffee as we people watch out the windows or around the shop. I'm not sure why I asked her to get coffee with me, but when I saw her on that sidewalk, I was desperate for a bit of normal conversation that I'd jumped at the chance. Or maybe it was because she'd been looking at me like I was diseased, like she'd caught me walking out of a murder scene instead of an AA meeting.

At that moment, I just wanted to show Ryan that I was a guy worthy of her time. And until now, I haven't allowed myself to think about what way I want her to think of me.

"How is the small-town life treating you?" I start with a basic subject.

Ryan shrugs, sipping her coffee. "It's fine, I guess. A change from traveling, but it's nice to be close to Presley for a while. I just taught a basic coding class to some middle schoolers at Hattie's insistence. It wasn't as bad as I thought it would be."

I take in her inky black ponytail, ears full of tiny hoops and studs, and the band of tattoos curling around her right bicep. Not only is she fucking sexy in an upscale biker chick kind of way, but she'd be one of those kick-ass teachers you remembered forever. One who was cool and let you call them by their first name, and you were actually excited to go to their class every day.

"That sounds good ... at least it gives you something to do

while you're staying in town," I tell her, not sure if she actually thinks it's a good thing.

Besides some errant gossip about a bad breakup, I know very little about why Ryan is staying in Fawn Hill. I suppose I could ask her, but she might take it as an intrusion, when we're really only at the surface level when it comes to knowing each other.

Aside from the fact that I've seen her naked. And she basically asked me to kiss her in the bushes during the manhunt party. Or that whenever we're within fifty feet of each other, I feel this electric tension stringing us together, as if we're connected by two ends of the same cord.

"So, do you ask all women you meet on sidewalks out for coffee?" She shoots me an arrogant grin, and I think she's flirting with me.

It's easier than getting into a deep conversation or asking each other personal questions. I know this game well, the one that's all charm and innuendo, rather than really getting to know someone. If this is how she wants to play it, I can do that, too.

As it stands, I'm kicking myself for even asking her to sit here with me.

"Only the ones who specifically know nothing about my sober journey but see me coming out of an AA meeting. Really freaks 'em out, ya know? That's what I'm going for."

"Shock and awe?"

"Or a sketchy past and a shaky future," I joke self-deprecatingly. "How about you? Do you always eat half an apple turnover with your best friend's husband's little brother?"

Ryan chuckles. "That's a stretch of an association. Can't we just say we're friends? I mean, you have seen me naked."

My cheeks definitely adopt a deep shade of pink. I've always been prone to blushing, and it has always annoyed the shit out of me. Something about it seems … unmanly.

"Fine, friends it is. Then we don't have to make this weird and call it a date." I try to keep my voice as humorous as possible.

Although, my cock would beg to differ. He has thought of dating Ryan in a very serious way, for a very long time. Probably from the first moment I saw her in that tight black dress at Keaton and Presley's rehearsal dinner. Her hair had been a spiky bob back then, and she'd looked so different from all the women I knew.

Like some ethereal, dark angel.

"I'm not dating men right now, anyway." She says it nonchalantly, but I hear the tension behind it.

I raise an eyebrow. "So, you're dating women?"

Ryan laughs, and I preen at how I just mixed her choice of words up. "No, although I might have better luck. No, I just mean ... I've promised myself I won't get into anything for a year."

For some reason, that makes me both relieved and irked. "That's good to hear, considering I'm not in the market for anything either."

As if she asked, dumb-ass. What the hell am I doing? I basically just told her that I wasn't interested in her either, as if she said it first and I was saving face.

"Oh, really? And why, may I ask, is that?" She lowers her mouth to the straw, sipping coyly as amusement plays over her features.

I realize that she's flirting with me, and I could answer with some charming, sly remark, but I choose to tell her the truth.

"When I got sober, there is this recovery rule that says you shouldn't start a sexual relationship within the first year of working the program. I took that seriously, and then I just extended it. I don't plan to start anything unless I'm completely serious about someone."

My answer puts a damper on the genial nature of our conversation, but I live my life owning my truths these days. Secrets keep us sick, that's what Cookie says.

"How long have you been sober?" she asks quietly, and I know she's probably been trying to work that question into the conversation for a while now.

"Five years. I got back from rehab shortly before Keaton and Presley got engaged, so I guess you'll never know crazy-party-animal me."

Most of me is glad about that. I was a mess as a drunk; sloppy and needy, always trying to be the life of the party even if it meant I'd break a limb. The things I said to women, how I treated them ... it was disgraceful. I'm happy Ryan will never have to witness it. Even if she isn't dating men.

"You should be really proud. It isn't easy overcoming addiction." She says this as if she has some deeper knowledge on the subject, and suddenly, I want to ask her how she knows.

My voice is low as I blink up at her. "Who says I've overcome it?"

Ryan nods. "You're right, that was the wrong word. Conquer? Tame?"

She isn't joking, and I can tell by the set of her caramel eyes that she's trying to congratulate me in a genuine way.

"Those are better. When you're an addict, there is no ... overcoming it. It's always right there, sitting just under the surface of your flesh. Most days, I feel like it's going to swallow me whole, and I only escape the pull by the skin of my teeth."

Hell, that was way deeper than I wanted to get. And now Ryan is looking at me with a timid, almost fawn-like indecision in her eyes. Should she stay and see if I put one right between her eyes? Or should she bolt, running far away?

I didn't think it was possible to scare a woman like her off. Apparently, I also had never voiced how difficult maintaining my sobriety was. And I'd just chosen the worst possible candidate to reveal the gritty, rough reality.

12

I can't fall in love with an addict.

Growing up in the clutches of one, I know how dangerous it is to trust them with your heart.

Shit, why the hell was love even on the tip of my tongue. I haven't even been on a real date with Fletcher Nash, and that coffee we shared after his AA meeting surely doesn't count.

Regardless, I'm on a fast from men. I told him as much. Not that it deterred his quiet, gentle, delicate soul from speaking directly to mine.

Fuck my foolish heart. It fell too easily and trusted too swiftly, despite its awful track record. My head wasn't much better, for as intellectual as I could be, my brain never talked the foolish organ in my chest out of the stupid shit it did.

It's been a week since my not-a-date date with Fletcher, and all I can think about are his words echoing in my head. That an addict never stops being an addict. His truth was so powerful, and ... refreshing. It was the first time in my life that someone who'd abused drugs or alcohol had been so upfront about what it felt like to suffer from the disease. And trust me, with my mother and growing up in the foster care system, I'd known plenty.

Our shared coffee drinking had ended awkwardly, with him trying to make some kind of joke to save us from the pit of reality he'd dug us down deep in. I escaped with half of my heart still lying on the table, listening to how damaged he was.

Because I was damaged, too, though my party trick was hiding all the scars and old wounds underneath a cool, composed, sassy exterior.

My phone chimes as I head into Kip's, the diner everyone in town seems to flock to for lunch. Presley asked me to meet her here, as we haven't gotten much time together with her busy studio schedule.

The message is from my boss, Geralyn. When I decided to move into consultancy, I wasn't going to pick just any company. I was going to pick the best, and one run by a complete badass woman in the STEM sphere. Geralyn Octon is such a woman and has no problem keeping up with the biggest of Internet bad boys. She works hard, is tough as nails, and runs one of the best hacker consultant agencies in the world. It's why I've been as successful as I am, picking her to be my boss.

Selecting the voicemail, I press my phone to my ear.

"Ryan, I just had a project come in with a big-time company, flashy data breach. Has your name all over it. Call me back."

A year ago, maybe even two, that message would have gotten my blood thrumming. I would have been like a dog biting to get off the leash to work on whatever project it was Geralyn described as flashy.

But at this moment? Nothing about her words excites me. I am so disinterested that I don't even feel like myself anymore. Something about Yanis, about Greece, sucked all the life out of me.

No ... I was lying to myself if I put all the onus on him. I'd been fading even before his betrayal. I am in my thirties now, and things I'd convinced myself I never wanted ... they've started to look appealing. Settling down, marriage, children ...

Why is it that I can practically hear the biological clock ticking in my ears, now?

"Hey, you!" Presley bounces out from the booth she's secured for us in the back.

The diner smells heavenly, like fresh peaches and sizzling, buttery pie crust. I'm in dire need of a thick, juicy burger, and my mouth starts watering for it.

"Hi." I hug her, kissing her on the cheek as we both pull away. "How were the morning classes?"

Presley hasn't even grabbed us menus. Probably because she knows I'll order a burger, and I know that she'll order a BLT. These were the little intricacies of knowing someone for as long as we'd known each other. In New York, we'd been family. I'd been the only one there for her, and while she knew a bit about my past, I wasn't sure she fully grasped that she was my *only* family.

She giggles. "Mr. Abrams farted again in the senior class. I had to try so hard not to laugh."

"Something about that downward dog really gets him barking." I wiggle my eyebrows, cracking the pun.

Presley rolls her eyes. "That one was too easy."

We order as the waitress comes by, who then asks how Presley is and if she and Keaton plan on attending the town hall dance in three weeks.

"Wouldn't miss it. Don't you know I'm married to the self-appointed mayor? I think Keaton is secretly hoping we win Mr. and Mrs. Fawn Hill." My best friend shakes her head as if her husband is incorrigible, but deep down, I know she thinks his childlike splendor about these things is adorable.

"This place really is something right out of Gilmore Girls," I tell her, sipping my lemonade the minute it's set down on the table.

"That's why I stay. Oh, and the fact that I belong here more than I ever have anywhere. Isn't it strange? Me, here?"

Honestly, when she first moved here, I thought she was nuts. I'd pegged it as just another Presley running away from her problems situation, and bet she'd be back in the city in two months' time. But now that I've met the Nashes and have stayed in Fawn Hill for extended periods of time ... I understood why she fit so well here.

My head cocks to the side. "No ... it suits you."

"The small-town vet's wife. I guess it does." Her smile widens, and I know she's mooning over Keaton.

"And the kick-ass yogi business owner who has transformed a town's fitness regimen. Give yourself the proper credit you deserve."

She nods. "I learned from the best, after all. Remember when you made me demand a raise at the restaurant I was hostessing at?"

The place had been a brown-nosing eatery close to the major news network buildings, used for schmoozing anchors and guests alike.

"Yeah, because they were giving you like two bucks an hour and made you close every night. I woulda socked that manager right in the nose."

Presley laughs. "And I did it, you got me so fired up. Then he canned me right on the spot. Said I was a cocky little bitch not worth my weight in martini olives."

"Well, at least he had a good comeback, that's one I'd never heard. Besides, you asserted your value. A woman should never underestimate it in business."

My friend reaches across the table. "And you never have. You're one of the savviest women I know. But honestly, I like that you're teaching at the middle school. It might be the best job I could have thought of for you."

I'd gone to the school yesterday, for the second time, and given a lesson on creating GIFs that the class was especially thrilled about. By the end, we'd made some hilarious video memes of their favorite cartoons or TV shows.

"It's not a job ... you get paid to do those. And don't lie, you never thought I'd be a good teacher. I'm not a kid person."

Presley rolls her eyes. "I hate when people say that. You're not *not* a kid person, you just haven't been around them much as an adult."

"I was around them enough as a kid," I tell her, an edge to my voice.

Her eyes soften a bit. "That was a different situation, and you know it. You're a cool woman, like one of the neatest people I've ever met. You're quirky and sarcastic, and you can talk to anyone in a way others can't. It's not a mystery why kids would be drawn to you ... you're like, who I would have wanted to be when I grew up if you were my teacher."

Our waitress sets down our food, and I immediately take a giant bite of my burger. The cheese blends into the meat, and the tang of the ketchup hits my tongue in vinegary goodness. Looking across the table, Presley is just as invested in her BLT. We're making sounds of ecstasy over our food, probably loud enough to attract the looks of other diners, and we both start to laugh at the same moment, mouths full of food.

"Being there just makes me think of how awkward I was in my middle school days. I had a hopeless crush on this guy named Tim. We were a couple for all of three seconds before he dumped me because he said I was too distracting with his youth football schedule."

"Stop it! Men never change, do they? Except now, instead of youth football, it's poker night with the boys. In middle school, I had not yet mastered how to tame my hair. I looked like a giant fuzzy monster, like Elmo if he'd been sent through the spin cycle."

A giggle escapes me because I've seen those pictures of her. It wasn't a pretty era for my friend.

"Would you go back? To the high school glory days?" I ask, wondering about her answer.

She tilts her head to the side, chewing a hunk of bacon as she considers my question. "Hmm, sometimes I'd like to. Life was so much simpler then. Homework had a deadline, Friday night parties were a guarantee. Your laundry was done for you and everything in the world was tainted with this hopeful possibility or something. Like anything was just in reach at the tip of your finger. How about you?"

It doesn't take me even a second to answer, "Not if you paid me a hundred million dollars."

Getting out of high school meant aging out of the system. It meant no one could keep tabs on my life anymore.

The past twelve years had been my glory days, and I'd lived them to their fullest.

"Fletch? FLETCH?"

Someone calls my name over the pound of the country song banging through the speakers in my shop. The chainsaw in my hand whirs and jumps as I slice chip after chip from the massive block of wood in front of me. I'm not sure yet what it's going to be, but my brain has been grasping at ideas all week and I've finally had time to come out here and do something about it.

I turn the belt off, waiting until the tool is all the way off before I set it on the ground. Prying my goggles from my face, I look to the entrance of the barn to see Keaton.

He walks in, admiring some of the half-finished work I've got going on, and sets a bag that looks suspiciously like the one from the donut stand on Main Street on my workbench.

"Brought some reinforcements." He nods at the pastry bag, and I open it to peer inside.

My favorite chocolate cruller and a Boston cream sit side by side. "Thanks."

I haven't spoken to any of my brothers since poker night,

which was about two weeks ago. It's the longest I've gone without talking to them since I got sober. Back when I was drinking, I would disappear for a month here or there, sleeping on friend's couches or scumming around with lowlifes. I've tried to cut out the isolating behavior since I came home from rehab, but I'm still pissed about what went down at Forrest's house.

"What are you working on?" My older brother sticks his hands in his khaki short pockets, and I know he's trying to lean into the conversation with softball questions.

"Not sure yet." I cross my arms over my chest.

I'm being glib on purpose because he wants this to be easy. Everything comes easy to Keaton, who has been the golden child of our family since my life started. I didn't even have a shot, Keaton is six years older than I am, and he'd already firmly cemented his role as the next in line to the Nash throne by the time Forrest and I came into the picture. Dad groomed him to be a mini Jack Nash, and so far, he was doing a bang-up job.

So, no, I wasn't going to make this easy.

"Come on, Fletch, don't be like this. I brought you a peace offering donut."

A frustrated breath escapes me. "You guys don't trust that I can live a full, sober, successful life. That's what it comes down to, Keat."

He shakes his head. "That's not it at all. We just ... we worry about you. I am so proud of how far you've come, but ... you didn't see yourself all those nights, Fletcher. Passed out on disgusting, sticky floors. I had to put you over my shoulder ... hell, countless times. Forrest got punched in the face, twice, for coming to your rescue over run-up bar tabs. Bowen's job at the fire department was in jeopardy when you lit those curtains on fire at that house party and almost burned down the entire neighborhood. We all love you, we're rooting for you, but we've seen some scary shit. You're our baby brother, we just want the best for you."

My anger rises two shades up my neck. "I'm not a baby, Keaton. I'm a grown man who can't live in a padded cell his whole life because I fucked up years ago. You all need to trust me way more than you do. I understand that I scared the crap out of you, and I've apologized profusely for it. But you also have to give me some credit. I've been sober for five years. I'm ready for a place of my own."

He considers me for a second and then nods. "I'm proud of you. And because you're not wavering in your determination, I'm even more proud of you. I know that you're a man, but ever since Dad ... died, I feel responsible for how your life turns out. How all of our lives turn out. That's all. I'm sorry, I really am. Now, eat your goddamn donut."

This is how guys operate, and I know it's the most sincere apology I'll receive from my brother, so I do as he says and reach inside the bag.

"Are we good?" Keaton says as I munch my donut, not having acknowledged his apology.

"Yeah, we're good. Although I might require one more of these before I fully accept." I'm being a brat and I know it, but it's nice to watch him squirm for a minute.

"Jerk. Anyways, there was another reason I came out, other than to stroke your bruised ego." He gives me a pointed look.

"And what's that?" I polish off the snack.

"The town council has been considering replacing the clock in the tower at the municipal building. It hasn't worked properly for years and just looks outdated up there. They want to put out a contract for it, and I mentioned to Gordy that they should reserve it for you."

Gordy's a childhood friend who now owned a landscaping

company in town and occupied a seat on the town council. My heart starts to thrum as I listen to Keaton's proposal, and I wonder how fate dealt such a perfect hand.

"Who told you I was working on a clock?" I muse, knowing Forrest had been flapping his big mouth again.

"Who do you think?" Keaton rolls his eyes sarcastically. "But seriously, you should do the job."

I drum my fingers on the workbench, ideas already fluttering around my head about how to build a brand new and improved clock tower. "Well, I don't want the job given to me ... I've done too many things in my life the wrong way. I'll bid properly, just like everyone else going for the contract. But ... anyone else will have a hard time beating my price. Because the money, any kind of it, will be better than what I'm working for now. And that's free."

My brother smiles. "That's precisely what I was thinking. Low ball them, make some extra cash, and then let your work speak for itself. Once people see this project, your name will start buzzing in certain circles. I think this could be huge for you."

I might not have seen it when he walked into my barn, but Keaton truly was proud of me. He wouldn't have put me up for the job with Gordy, or come here to convince me to apply, if he didn't want the best for me.

"All right, well, I have to get back. Seems that Hattie's dog, Chance, swallowed a roll of pennies whole. How that dog is still alive is beyond me ..."

His sandy blond hair, so different from the rest of our dark locks, shakes humorously as he goes to leave.

My voice stops him. "Hey, Keat?"

"Yeah?"

"Thank you."

He nods, and there is an understanding between us that I'm thanking him for much more than a donut, or suggesting I do some work for the town.

I'm thanking him for believing in me, even when I don't think he is.

Dark black satin hugs my body, and I know I will look out of place.

In the room full of sundresses and summer rompers, I'll stick out like a sore thumb. But I haven't had a night out in almost a month, and when you hail from the Big Apple, swanky lounges and cool SoHo bars are practically a multiple-days-a-week occurrence.

"Holy shit, you should be on the sparkly pink Victoria's Secret runway." Penelope wolf whistles as I walk into Presley's bedroom.

She and my bestie are getting ready for the town hall dance, lining the rims of their eyes with black kohl pencil and fluffing up their hair. In typical Fawn Hill fashion, the dance starts at five p.m. and goes until eight, so that some of the kids over the age of seven can attend with their parents. It's so out of my wheelhouse that I actually laughed at the flyer Presley showed me a week ago. This town and its adorable traditions.

I do a twirl, showing off for them. "I am going to stand out like a sore thumb, but I don't care."

Honestly, I've never cared much what people thought about

my appearance. I wear what I want, when I want, style my hair against the trend and am never far from my prized possession leather jacket. Compared to Penelope, in her floating yellow maxi dress, and Presley, in an olive green romper, I look like I'm ready for a gothic slumber party. But I feel hot as fuck, and that's all I care about.

"Oh, stop. Everyone in the place will be so fucking jealous of you, they won't have time to sneer." Penelope waves me off.

"There is going to be booze at this thing, right?" I cross my fingers, holding them up for the ladies to see.

Presley shakes her head. "No, unfortunately. Since it's at town hall, there is technically no alcohol consumption allowed on premises. However, it doesn't mean we aren't pre-gaming in the parking lot or sneaking water bottles full of alcohol in our purses."

"Very high school prom. I love it," I say, nodding with approval.

Penelope shrugs, pulling her boobs up a little higher in her bra. "We're leaving the kids at my mother's, so we have to get a little wild and crazy on our night off. Plus, we all haven't been out together in ages."

"Let's get started early." The twinkle in Presley's eye tells me she's ready for a night out, too.

She goes to her dresser, where I see a bottle of grapefruit vodka and three shot glasses sitting.

"Grapefruit vodka? Yuck, Pres. They really have turned you into Little Miss Huckleberry out here." My body shudders just thinking about the sour liquor I'm about to swallow.

Her eyebrows knit together. "Don't call me that. It's good, you haven't even tried it."

I may have struck a nerve, so I nod and walk toward her, accepting my shot glass. Penelope joins us, her beautiful blond locks piled into a girl-next-door ponytail that looks both chic and adorable. The woman is a knockout and has a better body than me after three kids.

"To Ryan. We're so glad you're hanging out in the sticks for a while," Penelope toasts sarcastically, and I give her a wry smile before knocking my shot back.

To my surprise, the taste isn't half as terrible as I thought it would be.

"See? It's good." Presley sticks her tongue out at me.

"All right, we better get outside. The boys and Lily will be here soon."

Lily was planning on getting ready with us, but then called last minute to say she'd do her makeup and hair at home since Molly was cluster-feeding at the moment. Penelope and Presley had nodded into the phone sagely, all understanding. I had no idea what the fuck a cluster-feed was, so I just went along with it.

The idea of walking to city hall from here, behind all the Nash men and their wives, was kind of intimidating. I was the odd girl out on their date night, and in my spiky heels, I felt even more so.

I hang back to go down the stairs last, with my two friends nearly bouncing out the door, waiting for their husbands to arrive. The boys all headed to Bowen's for pre-dance beers and bullshit, and I was kind of happy not to have them here when we were getting dressed.

It felt like the good old days when Presley and I would sit in our shoebox city apartment and do each other's hair or borrow a top from each other. The routine of girl gossip and makeup application makes me feel a bit more like myself ... something I haven't felt since probably before I went to Greece.

I'm just nearing the front door when I hear whooping outside.

"Damn, my wife is hot!"

That'll be Forrest, and by the time I push past the screen door, he and Penelope are full-on making out in the street.

"Gross, get a room." Bowen growls though he's holding Lily's hand like they might make a break for it. Being new parents can't leave much time alone in the bedroom.

"Hi, babe." Presley pushes up on her toes to kiss Keaton.

If I didn't feel thoroughly left out before, I sure as hell did now.

"Jeez, Ryan, you look great," Lily gushes as she comes over to kiss my cheek, holding my hands out to admire my getup.

She's in a lilac top and skirt set with little white polka dots all over it. She looks every bit the charming, pretty, conservative woman that she is. Lily is that girl in grade school that everyone wants to be. If this were Hollywood, she'd be the Reese Witherspoon of the bunch.

"She's right, you look wonderful." Keaton winks at me, and I know that my best friend's husband is only paying me a compliment because no one else is here to.

That's when I spot him, stepping out from behind where Forrest and Penelope are still practically foreplaying in public.

His eyes, the color of bright blue sea glass weathered by the ocean and time, connect with mine and almost smile. A shock works its way from my throat to my belly, and then all the way down to my toes. It's not a shock really, I shouldn't call it that. What I should say is it's a ... gentle slide of surprise every time I see this man.

I'm not sure that even makes sense, but each time I hold Fletcher in my gaze, I discover something new. Like I missed a piece of him last time I looked at him. What jumpstarts my system most, though, is that it's as if he's experiencing the same thing.

"Hey." He holds up a hand, and I see the calluses dotting each crevice of his palm.

"Hi." One shoulder rises as I say it, almost in a shy greeting.

"Let's get this show on the road. I have punch to spike," Forrest quips, and the group begins moving.

Fletcher and I fall to the back, in a natural step, as the couple's all walk arm in arm in front of us. The pairing off is something I expected, but I didn't have the balls to ask if Fletcher was coming, so I was semi-sure I'd be walking alone. The fact that he did come only heightens my nerves about the evening.

"Do you go to this every year?" I ask, trying to make polite conversation.

He shakes his head, dark locks of hair spilling onto his forehead. He's wearing a stark-white short-sleeved button-up, and it contrasts so vividly against his bronzed skin. Fletcher's complexion makes it look like he's been out working on the land, or something equally as small-towny. I realize, for the first time in the many weeks I've been here, that I don't really know what he does for a living.

"Not usually, no. But my brothers wouldn't get off my ass about it, and they said it would be rude for you to not have a ... date." The way he says it makes me think he's chewed the word around and around in his mouth. "Not that ... I mean, I came mostly because I'm bidding to win the new clock tower project and want to make a good impression on the town council. But don't tell them that."

The last couple of sentences whooshes out past his lips as if he's trying to erase the word date from between us. I follow his cue, pretending to zip my lips.

"I promise not to tell a soul. Not that I know a soul here to tell." I laugh nervously. "So, the new clock tower, huh? I didn't know you ... constructed things?"

I'm not exactly sure what to call it, or what he does to build something like that.

Fletcher grins. "Well, make things. I guess, you could call it that. Construction genus, I am not."

"I'm sorry, that sounded dumb. Please, forget how awkward I am with words and tell me what you do." There, that sounded a little more like I passed second grade grammar.

"No worries. I do make things, in the simplest terms. At first, it was some whittling to keep my mind, and hands, occupied once I came home from rehab. While I was there, I became obsessed with building those model ships. I guess from one addiction to the next, right? And then it turned into constructing bird feeders, or a stool. I remember I finished this thing my mom could hang on her wall, a shelving unit of sorts with baskets, so that she could put her keys and bags there when she walked in the front door. And I thought, 'wow, I'm actually not too bad at this.' So then, I made that piece for Presley and Keaton's wedding, and it just spiraled from there. People started requesting furniture or special orders ... and I make a decent penny off it now. But, I want to make it my full-time gig. The first step is moving out of my mom's house ... which is in the works. God, that probably sounds pathetic to you."

The way Fletcher talks about his addiction, so open and honestly, it freaks the shit out of me. I've been conditioned, from a very young age, to keep my demons and insecurities locked up tight. Those are the things that make us most vulnerable, the things people can take advantage of. Anything that breaks you down should live in the shadows. And don't even talk about the process of healing ... because it won't happen.

These are the principles I've been led to believe. I've never met anyone before Fletcher who completely shattered them.

"Honestly, I think it's something to be really proud of." I almost whisper this, and I can feel Fletcher turn his head to look over at me.

And without me having to say it, I think he knows that I'm not just talking about moving out of his mom's house.

"You think?" His voice is full of wanting to please me, to believe that what I've said is true.

I nod. "Trust me. Most people I've met in this life wear ego and fake niceties like permanent jackets. I find it refreshing that you wear your wounds as badges of honor."

15

Fawn Hill's town hall is a stately building and looks pretty much how you'd assume any small-town municipal building would look.

Red brick exterior, tall white columns in the front, the town's name in big, white bold letters over the front entrance. There are potted plants labeled as gifts from the elementary school dotting the sidewalk leading up to the double doors, and once inside, the whole place smells like a government office. If you're wondering what a government office smells like, it's a combination of Clorox wipes, laundry starch, moldy wood windowsills, and the musk of old library books. I find the scent oddly comforting.

Keaton leads the way through the winding halls of the building, and the group of us passes the courtroom, the mayor's offices, the entrance to the library, and other wings. Then we're at the dance hall, which is really just a bunch of recreation rooms that have their dividers lifted to make it one giant space.

"Wow, this place looks great," Presley beams.

I think she just hasn't been to the city in a while, but I don't say it. The hall is decorated in streamers, shiny cellophane, and tons of hand-drawn pictures that look like fourth graders drew them. It's all very small-town cute, but it isn't ... great. That makes me sound like an asshole, but I've been to clubs in the city that have four-story glass sculptures, go-go dancers in cages, and walls of speakers that almost blast your eardrums out.

This is just okay.

"Thanks. I haven't been back to work yet, but I had a hand in this," Lily brags, but it's just in the nicest way that no one takes it as boastful.

Bowen bends down to press a kiss to his wife's forehead. "You did an amazing job, babe."

"All right, who wants hooch?" Penelope pulls a flask out from the pocket of her dress.

"You brought moonshine? Where the hell did you even get that?" Presley looks shocked.

I'm just floored that anyone would refer to alcohol as hooch. I'm even more backwoods than I thought I was.

"That stuff will rot your stomach." Fletcher grimaces, like he knows all too well.

"But it'll get me drunk. And we are free of kids tonight. So I say go big or go home." Penelope takes a swig, sputtering as the drink hits her throat.

Her husband takes the flask, knocks one back, and then says, "This tastes like battery acid."

Bowen tries his luck next, always the manly man of the bunch.

Lily shakes her head, indicating a pass, and Bowen goes to hand it to me.

"Eh ... I think I'll hold off." I'm not sure I'm ready for something that hard ... especially in front of the kids dancing to One Direction right now.

"Fine. Let's go dance!" Penelope throws up her arms, and everyone follows their Queen Bee.

She's the morale of the group, the one who incites happiness and fun. As a mom to three boys, it amazes me how she does it. I feel like I would be hiding in a closet somewhere, having a breakdown.

The eight of us dance to Stevie Wonder, Tim McGraw, The Beatles, Rihanna, and a whole mess of other music. I have to admit, it's pretty fun. There is no judgment or lingering glances across the dance floor. There is no dark lighting or potent mixed drinks. No sleazy guys trying to pick you up.

Just some good old-fashioned fun at the town hall.

"We Danced" by Brad Paisley comes on, that soft, haunting melody spurring lovers to find each other's arms. I'm not sure how it happens, I'm fairly certain Presley practically shoves me from behind so that I tumble into Fletcher's arms. But ... here I am, the youngest Nash brother holding me as a slow dance starts up.

Amusement and something close to polite annoyance paints his face. "I guess I should ask you to dance?"

I swear, my face is ten shades of red at this moment. "I'm sorry, I didn't mean ... I think someone pushed me."

He seems to weigh this answer, and I can almost see the war playing out in his head. Should he really ask me to dance? Or would it just be too much of a hassle? Would it be rude if he walked off? Or does our holding each other during a love song register far more consequences?

Finally, the lines of his face settle in an answer. "All the same, you're here. We're both partnerless. Dance with me."

It's not a question, and against the logic trying to slap me in the face, I relent wordlessly. Fletcher's long, ropey arms hook around my waist, settling at the appropriate height on my back ... but the touch still makes every pore tingle. He's taller than I am, even with my sky-high heels on. And the solid mass of his quintessential male figure reminds me, as I press my breasts and belly to his torso, that it's been a long while since I've been to bed with anyone.

Then, right there on that packed hardwood floor, we begin to sway. I get a little lost in the lyrics, my mind swept up in how much this man really did fall in love at first sight with this woman. The sappy, lovesick damsel in me wishes that any of my relationships had been so hopelessly romantic.

Because that's what I am, a hopeless romantic. No matter how many times it scorns me, I will always believe in love. Even if I'm terrified of it, I'll never stop imagining that everlasting, all-consuming, genuine love can happen. And the songs about it only reinforce my rose-tinted view of it.

Fletcher's breath blows hot near my temple, and I try to contain the shudder that runs through me. My arms clasp around the back of his neck, and I can't help when my fingers trail over the soft hairs at the nape of his skull.

"So, we talked about my emotional demons last time I saw you. How about we cover yours this time?" He chuckles in my ear, his body and hands far too close to keep my brain thinking rational thoughts.

I'm almost glad that we're slow dancing, our cheeks almost pressing together. It means he can't see my face, or read my eyes in that weird, almost searching way he does.

"What do you want to know?" My voice has an edge of warning to it, almost as if I'm telling him not to test his luck.

Fletcher makes a humming noise, like he's thinking. "Why aren't you dating men right now?"

The phrase he uses has a small smile spreading over my face, remembering our non-date at the coffee shop. "I just came off an epic breakup. One that should go down in the history books as the suckiest relationship ender of all time. So, needless to say, I don't feel like a repeat."

I can feel him nodding as his fingers dig ever so gently into the base of my spine. My dress is basically a second skin, but I wonder, without meaning to, what his hands might feel like if there was nothing between us at all.

"How long were you with the jackass?"

The song meanders as Brad Paisley croons. "Who said he was a jackass? What if I was the one who wrecked it?"

"You weren't," he says simply, as if he knows the deepest parts of me.

Somehow, the conversations between us always become intensely deep. I don't know why; I've never felt this sort of magnetism to anyone else before. And it honestly scares the shit out of me that Fletcher Nash seems to have my number.

I sigh. "You're right. This time. We were together for a year and a half."

"Must have been serious, then," Fletcher remarks, and I think I hear a bit of surprise in his voice.

My shoulders rise and dip, considering his statement. "Yes, and no. I've been in years-long relationships with other people before."

I don't say it to brag, it's just a fact. And one that Fletcher needs to really grasp the whole picture. I am not an innocent party in what happened between Yanis and me.

"Oh, yeah? Tell me about it. Let the recovering addict who's never been in a long-term relationship, solve your relationship troubles."

"Well, Yanis and I were together for a year and a half. Before that, I dated a guy in New York, that I met at a Soul-Cycle class, for a year. I was in the best shape of my life. Before him, was this surfer in California for six months, but I ended it because he kept leaving to go surf shark-infested waters in places like Tahiti or Honolulu. There was the New York City boyfriend who I was with for almost three years when Presley lived with me. And before him, I dated two guys in college for a year each, and then had my high school sweetheart."

I say it all in a whoosh of breath because I don't want to leave any spaces between the syllables. It all makes me look so terrible, like the serial monogamist I am, that I don't want to explain it slowly. Better to rip it off, like a Band-Aid.

"Wow ..." Fletcher says, a little breathless.

"Yeah ..." I agree, twisting my arms a little tighter around his neck so I can pinch my wrist.

It's something I do when the nerves kick in so badly, when I feel the mask of confidence I wear begin to slip. Don't get me wrong, I'm typically the type of person who *is* confident. I give no warnings about who I am and tend to feel very little guilt about the decisions I make. Only when I find someone who I think can truly wiggle their way under my skin am I an anxious mess.

"Did you love them all?" he asks, and I find the question a little rude.

But I answer, "I thought I did, at the time."

I feel him nod and wish the song would just end.

"What's next on your list of projects to construct?" I ask, trying to throw him off this line of questioning.

"The clock tower," he reminds me, and I curse myself with how forgetful my nerves are making me.

"That's right. Any leads on a place to live?"

"My sponsor thinks she found me a place, she's taking me there in a few days. Honestly, I don't care if it's a dump ... I just need a space of my own. Living with your mom is a total turn off." Fletcher laughs because we both have already admitted we're bad with the opposite sex.

But I wouldn't know what living with your mom is like, at any age. If I had a loving one, I don't think I'd mind living with her now. Of course, that thought comes from my total abundance of mommy issues.

"Well, I hope it works out."

The song is coming to an end, and when he begins to loosen his hold on my waist, I feel the breath come back into my lungs. Except when he steps out of my embrace, I feel oddly … empty.

"I'll let you know. Maybe I'll throw a housewarming." Fletcher shuffles his feet.

I smile and turn without saying anything more.

I need to find Penelope. Some of that moonshine is definitely in order.

16

My hand wraps around my hard-on, knowing I shouldn't feed the temptation but being powerless to stop myself.

Jesus Christ, the way Ryan looked in that fucking black dress tonight ... I could have died just looking at her. Just combusted right there in the middle of town hall. It was a miracle I hadn't dropped her as we swayed to the music, that's how goddamn jumpy I was just being around her.

I give my cock a tug, not even bothering to undress or get comfortable as I slide the lock in place on the door to my bedroom. Fuck, I really need to get my own place.

Soon after Ryan sheepishly ducked away from me on the dance floor, I'd found the guys I needed to schmooze for the clock tower project, and then promptly hightailed it out of there.

I had been two seconds away from dragging Ryan out of that converted recreation room and into the abandoned library. The stacks had always been a favorite of Bowen and Lily's ... I figured I could borrow their spot for the night. It took everything in me to keep my hands in a decent place, to keep my mind sharp enough not to do something rash and hasty.

My blood thrummed in my veins all the way home, and I swear I had a middie by the time I stepped foot in the house. Good thing Mom was still at the dance herself, because a man needed some semblance of privacy.

Balancing myself on the desk just next to my bedroom door, I slap my free palm down on its surface and fist myself with the other. My dick is so rigid, a drop of pre-cum dripping down from the head onto my white-knuckled fingers, that I know this won't take long.

My pants are at my ankles, the bottom buttons of my shirt undone and pushed around my back to allow ample jack-off mobility. I've gotten good at this, tugging one out quietly, quickly. For the past four years, I've been the same teenager who had to avoid four brothers while stealing nudie magazines from under their beds to masturbate to.

Right now though, I close my eyes and think of Ryan. Of how steamy and electric the kisses between us would have been if I led her to the library. Of how I'd pin her up against the shelves, those legs that seemed to go up to her ears wrapped around my waist.

My hand moves rapidly, my breathing shallow in my lungs, as I weigh whether she'd let out breathy moans or quiet squeals. My imagination runs with the whispered moaning, and my balls begin to move in rhythm with the thorough stroke of my fist over my erection. They seize up and then relaxed with each downstroke as I think about removing the straps of Ryan's black dress with my teeth.

What would her skin taste like? Would she passively watch me ravish her? Or would her hands be pulling at my hair, tearing off my clothes? A little bit of both, I'd like to think.

I'm so close now, right on the edge of coming when I envision what pulling her top down would look like. From the outline of her skintight dress tonight, I could tell her tits were sizable. Fuck, I'd all but glimpsed them when I'd walked in on her in Keaton's guest cottage. Not Pamela Anderson big, but full and real enough that they'd jiggle in my hands. That I'd have a mouthful of nipple to work with.

All of a sudden, I'm coming with a harsh shudder, my climax seizing everything in my body and turning the world upside down. My come coats my hand, my cock tingling with a sensation that even the best of poets have yet to fit into just one word. My spine burns with release, my balls aching from the sheer force of it.

As I come down from the high, I realize I haven't felt this disoriented after jacking off in quite a while. Probably because all of my material has been Internet-based. But the sexual tension of imagining a flesh and blood woman who is only miles away ... fuck, it feels good.

Not as good as having her do this herself would be, but I'd needed this. Hell, I hadn't even fantasized about actually getting to the good stuff. In the scene that played out in my head, I'd barely bent my head to suck her luscious tits. That's how much Ryan Shea got to me.

Collecting myself, I head to the bathroom and wash up, then brush my teeth and slip back into my room. It's only eight p.m., but I'm due to meet Cookie tomorrow morning and want to be up early.

Sinking into bed, in nothing but a pair of boxer shorts, I'm still trying to catch my breath.

God, how I could have used some of that moonshine after our dance together. My hands ached to rip that flask out of Penelope's hands. I could practically taste the burn of it sliding down my throat. And now, lying in bed, staring at the ceiling, every part of me twitches to go out in search of a bottle.

This is why they tell you to focus on recovery, not relationships. Because everything surrounding the emotions of love and lust will drive you to drink ... literally.

It's only by pure exhaustion that I fall asleep, drifting uneasily into slumber as visions of Ryan dance in my head.

I meet Cookie the next morning, out in front of Carlucci's, the sole Italian restaurant in all of Fawn Hill.

My family has been eating here for decades, and my mom is very good friends with the owner. When Mr. Carlucci sees me through the window, he begins waving excitedly.

"Want to head in, or up?" Cookie asks, crushing the cigarette she was smoking out on the sidewalk with the heel of her boot.

It's almost eighty degrees at nine a.m., and my sponsor is wearing genuine leather cowboy boots that come up to her knee. Only Cookie could pull it off, but I'm sweating just looking at her.

"Up?" I ask, genuinely confused.

Cookie points to the windows above the restaurant. The Italian joint is in the block of shops on Main Street in a red brick building with traditional storefront bay windows. I've honestly never given much thought to the second level of this block of shops. A childhood friend's father had a law office up there that I knew about, and a local politician had set up temporary headquarters there one year. Besides that, I hadn't really acknowledged it.

"Mr. Carlucci turned the three spaces above his restaurant into apartments, probably two years ago. They're nothing fancy, but the rent is reasonable and he'll throw you free slices at the end of the night."

The notion of calling this home begins to blossom in my head. "All right, let's go up and look at it."

My sponsor leads the way, and even though she's a toothpick of a woman almost two feet shorter than I am ... her presence is bigger than anyone I've ever known.

Dingy floral wallpaper coats the stairwell, and it smells like butter and marinara sauce in here, but that doesn't bother me. When we step onto the second floor, there are three doors lining a narrow hallway, and Cookie pulls out a key and walks to the one marked 3.

"There is one other person living in number two, and the first one is vacant for now. The girl is nice, a twenty-something who left her Amish community a while back and needed a place to stay. Mr. Carlucci says she's quiet and keeps the public areas tidy, so she won't bother you much. Make sure you do the same."

"Who says I'm living here?" I ask sarcastically as she pushes the front door of the apartment open.

"Do you really have any other option?" Cookie levels with me.

I bite back the no on the tip of my tongue as we walk through the apartment. It doesn't take long; the thing is barely bigger than the first floor of my mom's condo. A small living room slash dining room, a galley kitchen that I could walk the length of in two steps, a bedroom, and one bathroom with a simple shower and toilet.

It's nothing fancy, every wall is builder's paint white and none of the appliances or cabinets are updated. But it's clean, and it's private. And I know that I'll be able to call it my own ... a home that no one else can tell me what to do in.

"I'll take it," I say with a definitive nod.

Cookie slaps me on the back. "I was hoping you'd say that. I'll have Carlucci draw up the lease agreement, and you can move in next weekend."

The whole thing is so fast, I feel dizzy ... but, in a good way. "Thanks for doing this, Cook."

"This will be good for you, kid. I'm proud of you. Having your own space ... you're ready. It'll give you more privacy, more independence. And it means you won't have to sneak girls into your mama's house anymore."

"You know full well there have been no girls." I furrow my brows.

She shoots me an annoyed look. "That's half the reason I want you to sign the lease on this place. Five years is way too long for a man to go without sex. Not even love, I'm not saying you need to find your soul mate. But you need to get laid, kid. Your shoulders are in a permanent slouch."

"Are you offering?" I clasp my hands together in a praying motion.

Cookie snorts. "You couldn't handle the likes of me."

Her comment brings my mind straight back to Ryan Shea on the dance floor of the recreation room, in that hotter-than-Hades black dress.

I'm not sure I can handle the likes of her, either. I know she'd never be attracted to a guy like me. Ryan has dated men from Greece, New York City, Italy ... guys who actually went to college. Her dating past was worldly, and she'd rubbed elbows with men who worked at the top companies in the world. These guys probably had penthouses and traveled first class.

Meanwhile, all I could afford was an apartment above the pizza shop on Main Street in the Podunk town I'd grown up in.

Fine, I shouldn't call it Podunk. I love Fawn Hill. This place centers me, and I have no desire to leave.

But when I compare myself to the big hitters on Ryan Shea's relationship résumé ... it's hard not to feel like a total bum.

Today isn't about her, though. This is about the next step in my recovery and making the life that resembles exactly what I want in this world.

"Maybe in another life, Cook."

I sling my arm around the woman who helped save me, and we walk downstairs so I can buy her a slice or two.

17

RYAN

I've been in Fawn Hill for almost two months when Presley finally broaches the subject I've been expecting her to ask about for weeks.

"When do you think you'll head back to New York?" she starts the conversation while we eat lunch together in her kitchen.

Keaton is at the office, and she has a rare break from the studio and decided to come home.

Instantly, I bristle. "Why, do you not want me here anymore?"

The wounded foster kid in me bares her teeth, ready to defend her already-damaged heart and get herself prepared to be thrown away yet again.

"No! Oh my gosh, I shouldn't have started off that way. That's not what I mean at all. I love having you here, we both do. You can stay here as long as you like. I just mean ... well, don't take this the wrong way. But ... you seem lost, Ry."

Turmoil rages in my gut, because she's right, of course. But I haven't put words to my complete lack of a plan, of a path, and I'm not sure I want to talk about it yet.

"I ... don't know. When I'm going back I mean. To be honest, New York hasn't felt like home in a long time. It used to, maybe because you were there. But now, nowhere feels like home. I was in Greece for so long that I kind of lost sight of my life, and now that my relationship is over, it feels like I can't just waltz right back into the life I basically abandoned. Not that I was even fond of the life I had before, I don't know, I feel like I'm not making any sense."

My friend sets down her fork, balsamic dressing dotting the napkin next to her bowl. "You don't always have to know exactly where you need to go."

A whoosh of exasperation blows out of my mouth. "But I usually do! From a young age, I've always been decisive. I know where I want to go, and I get there."

"I'm going to be honest with you now because I can see how much you're struggling with this. You may have been decisive ... but Ry, you never seemed all that happy with your choices when you got to where you thought you wanted to go."

Her brutal assessment of me feels like a sucker punch to the gut. It's harsh ... and I can feel the sting of tears threaten. All the years, and I never knew that's how my best friend viewed me.

Presley holds up her hands before I can talk, signaling that I shouldn't get defensive and cut her off.

"I'm not saying any of this to be mean. I'm saying it because ... for a long time, you were the stable one out of the two of us. I know I have a sister, but she's never felt like one. You're my sister, Ry ... and when we were living in New York, you were the one who seemed to have everything figured out. But after I moved here, and I met Keaton, it made me realize that you were just as lost as the rest of us. Your life has been difficult, so you run at the things you think will make you successful. Relationships, work, travel ... you throw yourself into them so that you don't have to stop moving. Because when people eventually stop, that's when the doubts and the whispers about what's really going on inside start. That's where you are right now. And honestly, I'm happy you are. You've been running for a long time, trying to avoid this feeling you're stuck in now. But, it's necessary."

Her words gut me at the same time they ring perfectly clear in my head. She's so right, it's painful.

What started as a normal little lunch in her kitchen has me now breaking down. My voice is stoked with unshed sobs as I talk.

"If I just kept moving, if I just jumped headfirst into every-thing ... nothing could hurt me. The faster you go, the less hurtful a brush against your armor can be. That's what I thought. So I loved hard, I stayed in these relationships that were so shitty. Why did I do that? And the travel ... when I was a kid, I barely had a bed of my own to sleep in. And then someone wanted to send me flying all over the world. I thought it was the most amazing thing. But I'd arrive, I'd say yes to every new adventure, and at the end of the day ... I felt so alone. After you left New York, I don't know. I kind of lost my mind there for a minute. So no, I don't really want to go back."

Presley gathers me into a hug, and I rest my head on her shoulder, suddenly exhausted from the past decade of my life.

"Life doesn't always have to be moving. Sometimes, you can just stand still. I came here to find the piece of myself that I could feel was missing, and I ended up getting way more than I bargained for. This slower pace of life or stopping completely ... sometimes it can lead to answers we didn't even know we needed. Take all the time you need. Explore what makes you happy, instead of what you think will make you successful. Keep teaching at the middle school, hang out with me, or do things alone. This town can be a medicine for your soul."

She's rubbing my back and all I can think about when she

says to explore what makes me happy, is I don't truly know what that means.

"You're a good friend, Pres."

"Only because I love you. And I'll kick the crap out of anyone who harms someone I love ... even if it's them doing it to themselves."

That makes me laugh, a watery chuckle escaping my lips. "Maybe give me a day or two before the bell for round two rings and you have a boxing match with my brain."

"Deal," she says, releasing me. "But I mean it. Stand still. Find happiness."

Could it be that easy? Was that the equation she'd followed? If so, I'd take her advice. Presley had stood still and found a life here that she could really be proud of.

That was all I really wanted.

"**B**e careful with that!"

My mother screeches as Bowen and Keaton drag a couch through the entrance to my new apartment and probably scuff half the paint off the frame.

"Ma, I don't know how else you want us to do this," Bowen grumbles, and you can feel the annoyance radiating off of him.

It's already been half an hour of my mother, my brothers, their wives, and the kids moving things into my new place. A couch from Forrest's old bachelor pad, my bed frame, mom's old kitchen table, and two other big pieces have been lugged up the stairs, past the lunch hour rush at Carlucci's. In my small galley kitchen, Lily is unwrapping the boxes of plates wrapped in my old high school sports T-shirts, and Penelope is scrubbing down the shower saying it needs a good clean.

I love them, and I'm so thankful they're helping ... but they're also getting on my last fucking nerve. They're everywhere, all at once, yelling and almost breaking things. Putting items in spots I don't want them to go, or drilling nails into the wall to hang art I haven't approved. Mom is doing that thing where she just sits in a chair and bosses people around, and my nephews are almost tripping everyone at least five times in one minute.

My teeth are fully gritted, my jaw aching from the pressure I'm putting on it, when Presley walks in.

"Who wants donuts?" she yells, holding up two big pastry boxes.

I can smell the fried dough from here, and my stomach rumbles. Relief washes over me, because what is more comforting than a chocolate frosted?

"Me! Me!" Travis, Matthew, and Ames run at her, and she catches them with her free arm, hugging them into her.

"Go get some paper plates from the pantry and I'll split them up," Presley tells them, and they rush past me.

Forrest and I have just brought my dresser up, and it's in the middle of the living room but that's not stopping me from unpacking plastic bins of my clothes and putting pairs of jeans and sweatpants into it.

Stopping, I rise to greet my sister-in-law. "Thanks for bringing those, I think everyone could use a sugar break."

She winks at me. "I could tell, even if I wasn't here yet. Our family is a bit much, yeah? I figured that morale wouldn't last long in this small of a space."

"Well, thanks." I make a *pshh* noise.

She blushes. "I didn't mean it like that! This place is great, I'm happy for you. I just meant ... seven hundred square feet is a tiny space for so many Nash's."

"Truer words have never been spoken," I agree.

We're about to head over to the table where my vulture family members are scarfing down all the good donuts when a knock comes on the doorframe.

"Anyone home?"

Ryan stands there, a bamboo plant in her hand, looking just as fucking perfect as she always does.

My cock stirs, reminding me of the fantasies it's been all too privy to when it comes to this woman. Jesus, I need to get a handle on myself, my nephews are in the room.

"You came." I smile at her.

She shrugs. "I figured everyone else was going to see it before the housewarming, why shouldn't I? Plus, I'm here to make sure Forrest doesn't fuck up your Internet installation."

I should have told both she and my twin brother that I'd already called the cable company to come hook that all up, but I wasn't going to look a gift horse in the mouth. Ryan had come to help me move in, and for some reason, it means more than anyone else being here. Probably because I threatened them all and reminded them of all the favors I'd done. She'd come all on her own.

And in a way, it showed that she was interested in ... whatever it was that was going on between us.

"Hey, you don't touch those cords. I'm going to wire it so he has the fastest Wi-Fi this town has ever seen." Forrest flips his middle finger up at her, and his stepsons cackle.

"Dad, you have to put a dollar in the swear jar!" Ames tells him.

Ames is the only one who is comfortable enough to call my brother Dad. Probably because he doesn't remember his real father, a soldier who was killed when my youngest nephew was only a year old.

"What? I didn't say a word!" Forrest holds his heart like he's wounded.

"Our kids are too smart for you. I agree, give us the dollar." Penelope holds out her hand.

"Kids, don't ever give your mother money. She'll spend it on shoes." He points his fingers at the boys as if he's teaching them a very important life lesson.

"They're going to appreciate the shoes a woman wears

when they're older." Ryan snorts, and I can't help my eyes skimming down her legs to observe the plain white Chucks she has on.

"She's right!" Penelope points at Ryan like she's just made the most valid argument in the world.

"What's that?" I ask, nodding to the plant.

She extends the small elephant figurine full of rocks with a bamboo shoot sticking straight up out of it. "It's tradition to bring someone a bamboo plant when they move into a new place. It's supposed to bring luck to your life in that dwelling. So I hope this one works."

I take the gift from her. "I hope it does, too. Thank you for bringing this."

The gesture is small, but the meaning is big.

Over the next two hours, we move the rest of the furniture in, get a majority of the boxes unpacked, and my apartment starts to resemble something lived in and semi-homey. Part of me can't wait until they all leave, so I can spend my first night alone in the first place I've ever owned, well technically it's rented, on my own.

"Fletch, why do you have hundreds and hundreds of DVDs?" Penelope asks, looking through one of the crates I'd brought with me.

Forrest cackles. "He used to be obsessed with collecting them. Would use any spare dollar he could to go to Best Buy in Lancaster and pick out the cheapest DVDs. They're not even good movies."

"*Dumb & Dumber*? *American Pie 2*? *Major League*? These are all idiotic teenage boy movies. My kids would love these, though they're filthy." My sister-in-law laughs.

"Ew, DVDs, Mom? Yeah, right. Those things are ancient. You couldn't get twenty-five cents for those on eBay," Travis tells his mother.

"Well, if that doesn't make you feel like an old geezer ..."
Keaton laughs, and all the adults nod in agreement.

"I think you saying geezer makes you older," I tell him,
shrugging my shoulders.

After we're done, everyone heads downstairs for the free
pizza I promised them. When I come back out into the living
room, Ryan is the only one left, and she's sitting at my desk. Her
fingers fly across the keyboard, and by the adorable way she's
chewing her lip, I think she's probably jailbroken my laptop,
gotten me access to restricted sites, and whatever else it is that
brilliant hackers do.

"You should have a website," Ryan says as she surfs around
my measly laptop.

I really hope I cleared the browser history. Nothing like the
girl you're crushing on finding porn in your Google search.

"Why?" I say.

She looks at me as if it's the dumbest thing I've ever said.
"Um, because you run a business."

Ryan referring to my art and furniture as a business is the
first time I've even thought of what I do as ... well, a business.

"If you got online, built a website, maybe opened an Etsy
store ... it could probably double or triple your revenue. I can set
up both for you at no cost. The friend discount."

She's right, I should have set up some kind of branding
months ago. Make it official, make it searchable. No business
made it without an Internet presence these days, and even if I
wanted to be a solitary island out there in my barn, it was stupid
not to establish at least minimal brand association.

Though my mind sticks on her words. The friend discount.

"The friend discount, huh?" I put down my keys on the hall
table my mom brought in and walk over to where she sits at the
desk in the corner.

Ryan's eyes slowly blink up at me, the color an intoxicating amber. "Yeah. For free. Also, I have nothing better to do right now, and it'll take me a day. You should thank me, you'll get a five-thousand-dollar website for chump change. All you have to do is buy me a slice downstairs."

I'm getting closer to her, without even realizing I'm doing it. One second, I'm halfway across the room, then standing in front of the desk, and now I'm almost brushing my leg against the chair she sits in. But damn, when she said friend discount, and with her sitting here, alone in my apartment ...

I like it. I like her, in my space ... no one else around.

For the last five years, I've fought every urge. I've swum in the opposite direction of my instincts, and the upstream stroke has robbed me of so many things. I can't do what feels natural, I had to give up partying and drinking in order to save my soul.

But this? Wanting Ryan Shea? That's something I just can't battle anymore. I don't want to. The pure animal attraction, with something deeper running through the center of it that I'm not ready to acknowledge ... that is one thing I can lose myself in without fear of losing myself.

Stepping fully into her space, I put out my hand, hoping she'll take it. Ryan looks nervous but lays her palm over my own, and I pull her up gently. The door to my apartment is open, and I can hear the muffled noise of the lunch crowd, including my family, down in the restaurant. It smells like cardboard boxes and mozzarella sticks, and the chime of the new clock on my wall alerts us to the fact that it's three p.m.

These are all the things I notice right before I pull Ryan to me and kiss her.

Because once my lips are on hers, I can't think. And I don't mean, I can't think straight. I really mean, I've lost all ability to connect rational thoughts.

Her mouth is warm and pliable, searching as my tongue slips in and begins dancing with hers. It's been five years since I kissed a woman, and at first, I can't find my groove. I'm fumbling and too excited, and all I want to do is grind every part of myself into her. It's kind of pathetic, but then Ryan shifts her angle and we click into place.

The meeting of our mouths is sensual, hurried, breathless, and ... *right*. It's just so damn right that I don't know why I've waited so long to kiss her. Ryan tastes better than any liquor, sweeter than smooth summer wine and spicier than cinnamon whiskey. It takes every muscle in my body to keep us upright, to stop myself from stumbling backward with her into my bedroom. Now that I've had a taste, there is no way I can't drink the whole bottle.

I'm an addict; stopping after the first drink is not possible for me.

Her hand comes up between us, and she pushes my chest until our mouths pull apart.

I'm still in a haze, half-drunk off her taste when I realize she's talking. "I ... can't. I'm not ... looking for this."

I must nod because Ryan's eyes are pleading for understanding, and the silence between us is tense and getting more awkward by the moment.

Oh fuck, how damn wrong I was. I should have been very afraid, terrified even.

Because it's completely possible I'll lose myself in this woman. And never get the old Fletcher back.

Another day, another class with my middle schoolers. Sometimes, I wish our summer course was more than once a week, because I'm beginning to grow restless without much else to do. My boss keeps calling, asking if I'd like some remote work, but ...

I don't know, I just can't seem to muster up the energy to want to do it. Working with the kids is bringing me so much joy, and I know that not one project she could pitch me could measure up to it. I've been trying to sit still, like Presley says, and only do things that make me happy.

But it's so damn hard. Not moving at a fast pace forces you to think, it forces you to open up all the ugly thoughts you shoved down in a box in the back of your brain, and sealed tight. You have to unpack the turmoil in you, and I've never been good at that.

What I do know is that I like teaching the computer course. I like going to yoga three times a week, especially since they're free. I've taken up walking in the mornings, all over town before a lot of people are up. And sitting under the stars at night.

That last one sounds cliché, but there is nothing like a

country sky at night. I've never seen so many stars, never had such darkness, with no artificial light sources around. It makes a person feel really damn small.

I'm halfway through a dusk walk, the AirPods in my ears playing some murder mystery audiobook, when I hear the clomp of feet behind me. It's not unusual, I'm walking around the lake slash reservoir at prime running hours. After work, but not too late.

A hand on my shoulder, though, now that startles me.

"Ah!" I jump to the side, thinking someone is pushing me or falling into me. It's one of those knee-jerk reactions where you kind of just freak out and flail your limbs because you're surprised but also disoriented with headphones in your ears.

"Ryan, it's me!" I hear a deep voice say over the voices narrating my audiobook.

I rip out my wireless earbud and whip around, my heart beating fast, to see Fletcher standing there. "Jesus, you scared the shit out of me."

"I'm sorry, I called your name twice." His lopsided grin has my eyes fastening on his lips.

My gaze doesn't stay there long, because the man is shirtless. I can't help the way my eyes run down his naked torso, along the lines of his pecs, the way a bead of sweat drips off one nipple. I've never been particularly drawn to a man's nipples, but hell if I can't stop looking at Fletcher's. My eyes drop lower, to his abs. They're not sculpted out like someone on a romance novel cover, but there are six defined bumps that are possibly even sexier than the ripped and toned muscles of a body builder. Just the peak of muscle underneath normal, human flesh makes him more approachable, which I think makes me more attracted to him. He's not the typical pretty boy, Roman god I go for ... there is a real down-to-earth quality about him.

Fletcher has the kind of chest hair that is sexy, without being too much, and it darkens in color as the trail of it slips beneath his waistband. He has on simple black running shorts and black sneakers, with wireless headphones around his head. I wonder what he's listening to.

"Uh-huh ..." He clears throat, and I realize I've been staring at him for far too long.

Tapping my one earbud to stop my book, I fight the furious blush working its way over my cheeks. "Sorry, just ... in shock I guess you could say."

He gives me a look as if to say, "yeah, about my body." Hmm, how adorably cocky.

"Again, sorry. I just saw you and didn't want to not say hi."

"I guess it would have been awkward if we were both running around the same lake without saying hi." A nervous laugh comes out of my mouth.

Also, because you kissed me in the most toe-curling way two days ago and I can't stop thinking about it. Which I do, right in front of him ... start thinking about it. I can tell he's thinking about it, too.

Lord, that kiss was good. It was the kind of kiss that warms you up from the inside out, like sitting in front of a fire on a cold winter night and allowing sweet, rich hot chocolate to fill your tummy.

"You pushed me away when I kissed you."

Another giggle bursts from my lips. "Talk about not making this awkward."

In truth, I was being a coward about it, and he was being more of an adult even with our three-year age gap.

I had pushed him away. The reaction my brain and heart had while Fletcher was kissing me ... it scared the crap out of me. It was enough that I thought he was the first decent man I'd met in ages, but then he had to go and kiss me into oblivion and ...

Shit.

I sigh. "I know I did. Fletcher ... I told you my dating history. It's not hard to make the assumption that I jump into relationships. I am the type of girl who practically lives with a guy after the first date."

"Well, my apartment is definitely not big enough for that." The joke has him smiling, and me giving him a glare.

"I'm serious. I don't know how to ... go slow. I'm not even sure I'm ready to try to date someone, when I don't even know what I want for myself."

Fletcher nods and then gives me a look that says he's going to level with me. "You may jump in too quickly, but I've never even jumped in. The longest relationship I've ever had was probably a two-month fling in high school where I only hung out with the girl with other groups of people. I've spent the last five years completely avoiding dating, so all I know is slow. Or should I say, my dating speed is like one mile per hour, the car is barely even rolling."

That makes me smile, because he's so good-looking and honest, it's a wonder how he's still on the market.

Fletcher continues. "I think we should stop ignoring this connection between us. There is that spark, and it's rare. Even I know that, and I haven't been in a relationship ... well, I think we established, ever."

"What I'm trying to tell you is that I feel that spark way too often. I can't trust that feeling anymore, because it always burns me."

He shakes his head, that boyish smile of his making my heart do a backflip. "Nah, I don't buy that. You might have been attracted to those guys, but you didn't feel the spark. Your mind has just convinced you that a certain kind of lust is that spark. Think about it, hard. Do you think about me the same way you did with those other men? When we're together, isn't it different?"

His questions hits me square in the chest, and I realize I haven't met this Fletcher yet. For the entire time I've known him, he's been the goofy, emotionally weak, work in progress. The baby of his family, the injured one that they worry about and who takes the crutch they've given him and leans on it.

But this man? He's wholly charming. Self-assured and giving me the business while he pulls zero punches. Shirtless, not to mention. He's my dream guy on a silver platter, and even though I made a promise to myself, I feel that resolve weakening.

"Maybe it is," I whisper, but we both know that in this case, maybe means definitely.

"Just give me a chance. We'll go slow. Snail's pace slow."

It could be the sweat dripping down his chest, or the way his denim-blue eyes sparkle in the setting sun, but a sureness swamps me, stealing every last inch of will power.

"Okay."

Just one word, but I feel my whole world go topsy-turvy.

I n the days after the town hall dance, I made my bid to the town council about the clock tower.

I got a call that they'd chosen my contract and would love for me to build it.

Not only does it pay, literally, to be a hometown boy ... but it helps that I probably bid thousands of dollars lower than the other builders in order to win this project. That, and they know I'll do a hell of a job.

So, for the past week and a half, I've been working on it around the clock. From sketching in the silence of my new apartment, to rendering concepts on the design software Forrest bought me for Christmas, to spending time out in the barn, picking out the perfect materials. The vision for it consumes me, and all I want to do is work on it.

I have a deadline of five months from now, but I feel like, with all the creative energy flowing through my veins currently, I could get it done in a week. I know that's not possible, there are mechanics to be worked out, and models to be shown and metal that will be welded over its frame ... but I'm just so fucking happy to be doing something I love and showing it to our town.

There wasn't a question where I wanted to bring Ryan for our first official hangout. I'm calling it that, because if I say the word date, I feel like she'll freak the fuck out. But I want to show her a side of me that not many people see up close, so that she feels more comfortable.

That isn't to say I'm not nervous as fuck as I lead her into the barn I use as my workshop.

"So, this is it ..." I say, my voice wavering with struggle as I shove open the red, metal barn door.

Ryan insisted on driving here herself so that we didn't ride over together. She can tell herself all she wants that this isn't a thing. But, we both know that the minute I helped her out of her driver's seat, and our hands touched, there was an electric current that sprang up between us and hasn't stopped since. My flesh can feel its proximity to her, and I don't miss the way she keeps rubbing the goose bumps off her arms.

"Wow, Fletcher ..." Her face, so foxlike in its shape, alters into an expression of awe.

While she's gazing at my pieces, I take the moment to study her. Her lashes are impossibly long, making her look utterly female, but with those sharp cheekbones, you know there is bite under the surface. She's wearing a fire engine red T-shirt and paired with the black shorts and her jet-black hair, she looks like hell on wheels. But there is a softness there, too, one she's only let me get glimpses at.

"You built all this? I'm ... well, damn I'm so impressed. You're really good."

Ryan moves around the barn without permission, though she doesn't need it. Once I let someone in here, they can look at whatever they like.

Her delicate hands run over a few chairs I'm in the process of staining, she takes a look at the drawings for the clock, has a glance at some tiny soldier figurines I'm making for the boys, and then moseys around just taking it all in.

"It's a true talent that you can do this. Most people have no creativity in their brains. Me included."

I wave her off. "I'm okay at working with my hands."

It comes out as more of an innuendo than I meant it to be, and Ryan's gaze is pinned to my hands.

Quickly, I recover. "People's brains just work differently. Some would say what you do is an art. I'm hopeless with computers, Forrest keeps trying to get me to set up a Facebook page and it scrambles my mind."

Ryan's lips stretch into a smile. "I guess you're right. Take Lily for example, I'd never have the patience to put up with annoying library patrons all day."

"I can second that." I nod.

A ringtone chimes up between us, and Ryan reaches hastily into her pocket. One look at the screen and she silences it.

"So, can I play with a saw?" The expression she wears is downright trouble.

But damn, is she sexy. "I think we'll start with sandpaper. I didn't bring you here to have any fingers cut off."

We focus on one of my chairs, sanding the rough edges.

Her phone begins to ring for the fourth time since we came out here, and her face gets tighter with every call.

"Do you need to get that?" I ask, wondering if it's her ex.

The way she's staring at her cell, as if it might jump out and bite her, I'd bet it is. No one gets that look if it isn't someone who has scorned them or someone they deeply don't want to talk to.

"No. It's just my mother." The way Ryan says this, you'd think it was the grim reaper calling her.

"Are you two ... close?" I'm not trying to pry, but it seems like the next logical thing to ask.

She shakes her head, her eyes distant. "No. I grew up in foster care."

Shock works its way from my chest to my gut. "I ... didn't know that."

I'm not sure if I should tell her I'm sorry? I'm not really sure what to say, because I've never encountered someone who grew up in foster care. For all of its good qualities, Fawn Hill is not exactly worldly. The majority of the residents are made up of heterosexual couples who have two kids and the white picket fence. We don't have a lot of crime, or outsiders, and for that, I do feel I've missed out on a lot of the world. It's a wholesome place to live, but it doesn't detail the experience of many people living in our country.

"Yeah. I don't talk about it much." Her voice is clipped. "Anyway, what is this?"

Ryan is changing the subject, and we both know it, but I let her. If she doesn't want to open up about it, I'm not going to force her.

Moving to see what she's looking at, I find the piece I'm trying to design for Mom.

"It's a family tree for my mother. I'm trying to make it a little abstract, for a large wall over her couch that she's kept empty since she moved in."

"It's really beautiful," Ryan says quietly.

I've whittled and carved a large oak tree from a beautiful slab of oak. All the branches have a member of our family's name on it, with wooden leaves carved for the offshoots of their individual families.

"You don't have anyone on your branch," she points out.

I shrug. "Never met anyone to carve into it permanently."

"Why is that?"

I knew this question was coming, but the potential pitfalls of the answer leave me anxious. I haven't bothered to get close to a woman in five years, so admitting the disgusting ways of my past is something I haven't had to face. But, if I want Ryan to put stock in our connection, if I want her to feel able to talk to me, I have to talk to her.

"I started drinking from the age of about fourteen and didn't stop until I was forced to go to rehab by my family. In high school, it wasn't all the time ... until probably senior year. I'd show up drunk to class, to baseball practices, and if I wasn't at those places, I was loaded. But, as I came to find out, I'm an alcoholic. A highly functioning one. I could have five shots of tequila and talk to you as if I was as sober as a priest. No one thought anything of it, at first; my friends and brothers just thought I partied harder than them. But then, it started consuming my life. I couldn't get out of bed without drinking a beer. I couldn't make it through a day without ten drinks under my belt. After high school, I just lapsed into this junkie lifestyle. I was messing around with drugs, though alcohol was always my wife. She was the love of my life, and I was blacked out for the early part of my twenties. I'm not even sure who I slept with, or where I ended up at the end of the night. Half the time I had it, I wasn't even really conscious of having sex. That sounds disgusting, horrifying ... but it's true. I was so wasted, I don't even remember those girls' faces."

Ryan bites her lip, and I wonder if she thinks I'm a monster.

But, I continue. "When I finally got sober, they tell you in AA that you're not supposed to start a romantic relationship during your first year in the program. The focus is supposed to be on recovery, not a relationship. So I followed the rules, to the letter. I cleaned up my life, made amends to my family and those I'd hurt, started showing up for work and saving my money. And then ... I don't know. I just kind of let that no romance rule bleed into the second year, and then the third. I figured that eventually, if I was into someone enough, I'd break the dry spell. But that person never came, or maybe I just wasn't open to it. I focused on my family, my job, and my dream of turning all of this into a full-time gig."

When I finish, she's looking at me with a curious expression on her face. "So, when you mean dry spell ... you mean, you haven't ..."

"I haven't had sex in five years." I nod, fully aware of how pathetic that sounds.

What she does next right about bowls me over.

Ryan steps into my space, presses her palms to my cheeks, and pulls me in for a kiss. As if it's a Pavlovian response, my hands seek her hips, pulling our bodies as close together as they can be and then running up the length of her slim torso. I feel her shiver, and I walk us backward until I can lean against my workbench, the hottest woman I've ever laid eyes on pressed up against me.

"You are captivating ..." I whisper into her mouth, seconds before our tongues meet.

Ryan purrs with delight as our mouths dance. You can kiss anyone, it's just an action that most grown adults are practiced at. But for it to matter, for there to be passion, the person on the other end has to incite wonder in you.

And that's what this woman does for me.

I'm about to let my hand wander under her shirt, chancing my luck to see if I can move us any further, when Ryan bypasses all the bases and sinks to her knees.

"What are you—"

The words that come out of my mouth are hoarse and cut off when she deftly unbuckles my belt, unbuttons my shorts, and pulls down my zipper.

"*Holy fuck,*" I murmur, just the sight of her before me enough to have my dick ramrod straight in two seconds flat.

Ryan's long lashes sweep up, those whiskey-colored eyes

intoxicating to me. There is a bit of a devilish smile twinkling in them, and I'm seeing the temptress side of her. Everything about this woman is arresting, and now that I see her in the midst of her sexual prime ...

I can see why men fall at her feet.

She keeps her eyes glued to mine as she pushes my shorts past my hips and then reaches into my boxers. The second her fist grips me, I feel my knees buckle. It's been so long since someone other than my right hand grasped my cock, and the feel of her silky smooth fingers is enough pressure to make me come.

"Ry—" I want to tell her I'm not going to last even another ten seconds, but before I can get the words out, she tests out her grip and pumps a small stroke.

Her eyes go wide as they take my dick in, the length of me swollen and ruddy. The muscles in it twitch and make my appendage bob ... it's probably damn excited it's getting some attention after all this time.

"Wow," Ryan deadpans, and I have to puff out my chest a little.

Yes, back when I used to get action on the regular, I did have a little reputation. Or a *big* reputation, I should say.

"I mean ..." She trails off again, bringing her hand up to rub across her jaw.

"You're killing me, Ryan." My eyes go skyward, because I'm about to pass out with how hard my heart is beating. "If you don't want to, I didn't bring you here thinking anything would—"

"You haven't been with a woman in five years, Fletcher. I think you're way overdue for a good blow job."

I swear, I could blow my load just from her words alone.

When she wraps those plump red lips around my cock, though ... sweet lord have mercy. I might just die on the spot. Go into heart failure from the single greatest sensation I've felt in my entire life.

Ryan bobs up and down, sucking and pumping in a rhythm that makes my ears start to ring. I feel like I might fall over, and I'm trying to count to ten or tighten my ass cheeks to keep from coming too soon. I'll be mighty embarrassed if I can't last more than ten seconds.

But then she pulls me out of her mouth and runs her tongue along the underside of my shaft while kneading my balls in her other hand, and I know I'm a goner.

The minute she swallows me again, my cock halfway down her throat, I make a garbled attempt to tap her on the shoulder.

"Ryan, I'm going to, fuck ... I can't ... fuck ..."

It feels like my whole body is exploding as I empty into her mouth, this woman just patiently taking my come instead of moving to the side to jack me off. Euphoria runs through my veins, and I have to white-knuckle grip the table behind me to keep from collapsing. The goddess before me has completely undone me, mind, body, and soul.

She can't know how wholly she just blew my mind. What she did was selfless, it showed care for me in a way not many others did. Some might laugh at that assumption, because she'd just sucked me off, but it was, in fact, a significant gesture. She felt serious enough about me to take care of me, to give me something I've been depriving myself of.

And I was serious enough about her to let her do it.

Ryan stands, a cocky smile on her face, and I grab her, pressing my lips to hers. It might be a shock because she goes rigid for a minute. The thought that she's probably been with assholes who won't kiss her after a blow job crosses my mind. But I'm not that guy, and she just made me feel incredible. I want to thank her for it.

"That was not a nice blow job," I choke into her hair, still unable to feel most of my extremities.

"Way to make a girl feel good." I can feel her pout against my neck.

Air still evades me. "That was fucking spectacular. World ending."

Ryan pulls back, grinning from ear to ear. "Now that's more like it."

Molly gurgles as I bounce her gently on my knee.

"Her neck is so freaking strong, dude. Look at her holding it up," Bowen tells me this as if I know when babies are supposed to do this.

But he looks so proud, I nod. "Yeah, man, she's the most advanced baby in the game. Aren't you, little fart machine?"

My niece cracks a half smile, one of those adorable baby almost-grins, as she lets out a massive fart in my lap.

"Holy crap ... literally." I have to hold my breath, because it smells like a bomb just dropped in Bowen's living room.

"Ah, man, we might have an explosion." He quickly takes the baby from me and carts her off upstairs to deal with whatever is in her diaper.

I lean back on Bowen and Lily's couch, looking around the house that my brother used to live in alone, but has now given design control of to his wife. Their house is what I'd want, if and when I settle down. It's all neutral colors and comfy furniture, with pictures of the family everywhere. Presley and Keaton's house is a little more whimsical, what with her taste in eclectic art ... and Fletcher and Penelope's house is a mix of turquoise and yellow, with more pops of color. I feel like I'm on a funhouse ride in their house, but they love it.

My big brother comes back downstairs, Molly in his arms, sucking on her pacifier.

"Never thought I'd get satisfaction out of counting another person's shits for a day, but I guess that's fatherhood." His smile is dreamy when he looks down at his daughter.

"Do you like taking care of her when Lily isn't around?"

The girls are having a ladies' night tonight, leaving all the men at home. Ryan had joined them; I think they were going to the Goat for drinks.

"Hell, yeah. It's fun. And it makes me feel useful, being able to care for her all on my own. Plus, makes me look like a badass to the wife. Then she wants to kiss me even more." He winks at me, and I find it hilarious how Lily has turned him into a lovable Mr. Mom.

"Well, I'll plan to get out of your hair then, before she comes home." I snicker.

"So, what's up? Why are you hanging here and not at Forrest's?" he asks, flicking the TV on and turning to the base-ball game.

I check the score on the screen. "What do you mean? He's not the only brother I like."

"Yeah, but the whole twin thing, you guys are psychic butt buddies." Bowen says this as if it's fact.

I guess it kind of is. "Whatever. I wanted to hang with you. My big Bowie."

The nickname jab is because he called us psychic butt buddies, and I get the response I want when my older brother growls.

"Don't call me Bowie. And cut the shit. Tell me why you wanted to come over, other than to snuggle my adorable daughter."

Shit, he does see right through me all the time. See, Bowen and I are similar in a lot of ways. While Forrest is my twin, he's also very unlike me. Forrest is a grade-A brain and loner, he can spend days not talking to another person. He's always been on the outside of things, doesn't like sports much, and if he has a problem with something, he will confront you about it.

Bowen and I, we're much more internal with our feelings. Bowen more than me, but we keep things bottled up. To the point that they fester and begin to infect us with rage or hurt. I saw him do it with Lily; he lived in this bubble of anger for a decade and wouldn't get out of his own way to solve his pain.

Before I got sober, I was the same way. I used partying and being social as a cover for the larger problem that was eating me whole. And since giving it all up, I've used celibacy as a crutch. If I don't have the turmoil of a relationship, I don't have to worry that a fight or a financial commitment to someone will escalate into me having a drink.

I decide to broach the subject with Bowen, though I know he may crack some wiseass remark.

"How did you, uh ... stay away from Lily? Or when you knew you wanted to break your whole sullen and damaged routine to get her back ... how did you do that?"

"You're sleeping with Ryan, huh?" Bowen doesn't even bother looking at me.

"What the ... no!" I try to sound offended or surprised, but I know my older brother is looking right through this defense.

"Don't lie, Fletch. You're shit at it since you got sober."

I can't argue with him there. "Fine. We may have ... done something, but we're not sleeping together."

"You want to sleep with her, though, right?" Why does he have to be all up in my business?

"Yes," I grumble reluctantly.

"Glad you're finally admitting it. Forrest and I were taking bets on how much longer you were going to follow her around with your tail between your legs." He chuckles.

"You guys are fucking assholes."

Bowen rocks Molly, who is now snoozing in his arms. "Hey, language. There is a little girl present."

"Sorry. But can you just be serious for a minute?" I feel like a pouting school kid.

"You really like her." It's not a question.

But I answer it anyway. "Yes. I do."

"I didn't think you two had spent much time together," he points out.

"We've ... gone on two dates so far. But, I've known her for years through Presley. We've talked. And of anyone, I think you'd understand that there is a connection you have with some people that is just unexplainable."

My brother nods. "What's the problem, then?"

"I'm not sure I know how to be with someone. Or how to introduce someone into my life when there are so many rules I have to follow to stay on the straight and narrow. How did you ... how did you get over your shit?"

"I finally pulled my head out of my ass and realized that I could either keep living life as a sullen, dark asshole ... or I could go get my girl. I could stop being afraid of what would happen and be with the woman I loved since the first time I laid eyes on her. You just have to get over the mental hurdle in your head that says the world is going to end if something bad happens between the two of you. Are you going to fight? Are there going to be tough days? Will money be tight, will you both be tired? Hell fucking yes. But that's life, with or without her. And if she makes your world better, you best stop being an idiot and get over yourself."

Well, there was a Bowen pep talk if I ever heard one.

"Shit, I wish I could have a drink right now. Beer helps you mull things over, you know?"

Bowen looks at me like I might go postal and raid his kitchen for a drink. "Are you okay?"

I sigh. "Yes, Bowie. I'm fine. It's good to talk about cravings, or urges. It's better than bottling them up." At least that's what Cookie says.

"I guess that makes sense."

"I just mean ... thanks for the advice. I wish I didn't have to weigh every decision in my life so seriously. Like everything I do is going to tip the scales and send me sliding back down the bottle again."

My brother claps me on the shoulder. "Man, you have five years under your belt. You're doing a great job. We're all really proud of you. But if you don't get your head out of your ass and go after that girl, I'll give you a wedgie myself."

Brothers, am I right?

"You went out with Fletcher, didn't you?"

Penelope is about four beers in, and she's flying high on the alcohol buzz and a night off from mom duty.

I collapse into a fit of giggles, my head hitting the bar in front of me as I dissolve into my hiccupping laughs.

"Well, once. Technically. The other time was just a hangout, that ended in a blow job."

My hand slaps against my mouth because I can't believe what just slipped out actually slipped out. Those damn tequila sunrises were making my tongue even looser than it usually is.

"Oh. My. God!" Presley screeches, causing almost every patron in the bar to turn their heads and stare at us.

"Fuck you, alcohol," I curse at my glass, eyeing it with a glare.

"I ... I'm speechless ..." Lily's mouth is hanging so wide open, I could throw ping-pong balls in there.

"Is it incest that we all love Nash men and are therefore all attracted to the same look of a man?" Penelope snickers into her beer bottle.

"Ew, what? No. Bowen looks nothing like the other brothers. Neither does Keaton. The only two who look alike are Forrest and Fletcher." Lily scoffs.

"Well, duh, Lil, they're twins. Guess that means we're Eskimo sisters." Penelope elbows me.

"That's not what that means!" I cackle.

She frowns, her drunken brain confusing her. "No, you're right, I'm definitely getting that wrong."

"That's definitely wrong." I laugh. "Being an Eskimo sister is when you and a girlfriend sleep with the same guy, not at the same time though and not in a mean way. Like, if I had a hookup with a guy, and then you went on to have a one-night stand with him. But we both didn't care and were just weirdly psyched that we now had a bond about sleeping with the same guy."

"If you sleep with my husband, I'll kill you." Penelope points a finger at me.

I almost spit out my tequila drink. "Girl, I'm not going after Forrest. Believe me, the guy annoys the shit out of me. Love him, but he codes websites all wrong."

"No, you're just going after Fletcher. Can we please not lose sight of what's important here?" Presley bursts out, I think finally getting her voice back after I stunned her to silence.

My cheeks flame with a blush. "What's to talk about?"

"Um, you blew him!" Presley throws her hands up like I've lost my damn mind.

"The guy hasn't had sex in five years. He was in dire need." I shrug.

Penelope slaps her hand down on the bar. "I knew it! I knew he was dry as the Sahara. Damn, if I had to go that long without sex ... jeez, I went about a year and it almost killed me."

"You don't want to know how long I went, then," Lily mumbled. "Though that situation has more than rectified itself."

"We know, you have a baby." Presley eyes her sister-in-law, but I don't miss the edge of envy in her eyes.

It's not the time to touch on that, though I store it in the back of my brain for later. Maybe when we're not halfway down the bottle.

"So, you said you technically went on an actual date?" she presses me.

I sigh, knowing I shouldn't have let my big mouth blab, but also glad I can talk to them about this. They all know Fletcher more than anyone and are also three amazing women. I'm terrified that I feel such a strong connection with Fletcher ... and that I've technically broken my vow to myself.

"Yes, he took me to see his barn. So we ... hung out there and things escalated. And then two days ago, he took me to his favorite Amish country market."

"Ah, he got you with those apple turnovers, didn't he? What a great move. I'd sleep with someone if they bought me one of those heavenly pastries." Penelope tips her beer, seeming to compliment Fletcher.

That makes me chuckle. "It's like a food orgasm. Anyways, the date was ... good. Really good. But, I swore I wouldn't date anyone. At least not in the near future. And by near future, I meant forever."

Lily shrugs. "So? You like each other, you have chemistry. You should follow your heart."

"Says the girl who waited for a man for ten years. You're such a romantic, Lil," Penelope teases her best friend.

Lily rolls her eyes. "All I'm saying is ... life is short. And if you feel something for a person, you should go for it."

"That's my problem, though. Always has been. I jump into relationships and then spend years of my life with the wrong person because I think I have a *feeling*. Feelings are bullshit."

"Nahhh. Feelings are everything." Presley smiles at me. "You knew me before I met Keaton. I couldn't make a decision about anything. If a guy even mentioned commitment, I was bolting in the other direction so fast, he couldn't even finish his sentence before I was gone. But, then I met the sexy vet ... and it was all over. I just ... *knew*."

"That's what everyone says. All married people throw out that bullshit line like us single gals are supposed to understand what that means."

"It's true, though." Lily nods sagely.

"And I can attest that, sometimes, it takes a lot longer than you thought it would. But in the end, you just *know*." Penelope makes three.

Presley continues. "I know you. You feel differently about Fletcher. I could tell it the moment you guys met at my wedding."

It's my turn to roll my eyes. "Have you been talking to him? Because he said the exact same thing."

"Oh, just go for it, Ryan. Nash men are great in bed. We should know." Penelope hails down the bartender to order another round.

With the size of Fletcher's dick, I'm not surprised. I almost say that out loud, but the alcohol hasn't completely swamped my brain.

"We'll see."

"Seriously, don't wait ten years. You might live with regrets, but at least you acted on your feelings. That's better than not acting at all." Lily tips back the last of her glass of wine.

Maybe she was right. At the end of the day, what was another failed relationship to add to the pile?

Off-key singing meets me in the hall of Fletcher's apartment, and I pause to listen to it.

From behind the door of apartment number 3, the guy I'm quickly developing feelings for is singing "My Girl" at the top of his lungs. His rendition is not great, but he's giving it his all, and I find it adorable.

My heart also begins to flutter at the thought that he is singing that about *me*.

It's our third date in two weeks, and I'm not shying away from calling them that anymore. When you're spending time alone with a man, whether it's going out to eat or giving him oral sex in his workshop ... it's a little bit more than hanging out.

Yes, I blew him on the floor of a barn. And it was the hottest fucking thing I've ever done.

It was impulsive, and at the time, I was acting on instinct rather than logic. This is one of the sexiest men I've ever met, in an understated way, and no one had touched his cock in five years. That just seemed wrong to me. So, I righted the problem.

Watching Fletcher Nash come undone because of my touch, my mouth ... fuck, I have to rub my thighs together just thinking about it. The prickling friction I desire in between my legs is at the forefront of my brain when he swings the door open.

"Hey," His smile is easy, and he pulls me into a hug.

Gosh, he smells good. Like cinnamon and mint in one big, beautiful manly package.

"Hi." I press a light kiss to his cheek in a spur-of-the-moment decision.

Fletcher kissed me after our last date. Not that the kiss had been our first, or the date, technically. But it had felt like it. He'd done it in Presley and Keaton's backyard, just outside my door to the guest cottage. All slow and gentle, placing his hands on my cheeks and coaxing me in for a gentle caress, that turned into a simmering, smoldering kiss. I'd felt like we were high schoolers, sneaking in our first bit of making out before mom and dad turned the porch light on. It was the perfect end to a pretty awesome night, and I went to bed with butterflies bigger than any I'd felt before.

"Wow, this place looks so good …" I break away from him, entering his apartment without his invite.

Behind me, Fletcher chuckles and says, "Come right in."

"You've really done a lot, Fletch." I use the nickname without thinking, but it feels right rolling off my tongue.

In the two weeks since we moved him in, he's hung some cool wall art, gotten a rug for the living room, and set the kitchen table with a decorative wooden centerpiece I'm sure he made. Peeking into the bedroom, I can tell that the mattress and box spring are no longer on the floor but encased in a cognac tufted leather frame with a matching headboard.

"I like to think it looks more sophisticated than your average bachelor pad." He pats himself on the back.

"And that smell …" My stomach grumbles and we both laugh.

I hand him the bag with a loaf of crispy, crunchy Italian bread, just like he asked me to pick up.

"Oh, this is perfect, thanks. Have a seat and I'll serve us."

When Fletcher asked if I wanted to come over for dinner, I got a bit nervous. Having a guy cook you dinner, alone in his apartment, it felt like fifth or sixth date territory. But then he clarified that he wanted to do something special for me and have me as his first guest at his new place ... and I'd melted. It was a really sweet gesture.

Fine, my rose-tinted glasses were completely on, but Lily Nash had told me to jump in and she was the most conservative person I know, so I was following her advice.

The bread is in his one hand, and he laces his other through mine to lead me the short couple of steps to his table. It's romantic, and I notice when he's pulling out my chair, that he's set two candlesticks in the center. There is a new white tablecloth draped over the surface, and he's already set down plates and utensils.

"This is fancy." I give him a sarcastic smile.

"Only the best for Ryan Shea." His big hand squeezes my shoulder before he retreats to the kitchen.

My heart races with anticipation, because this is our third date. You know what they say about the third date.

"So, you cooked all this?" I ask, trying to distract myself.

"I mean ... I may have gotten Carlo, the chef downstairs, to give me a couple of tips. And his special marinara sauce, but you knew I wouldn't make that from scratch."

Carrying two plates loaded with spaghetti and chicken parmesan, Fletcher sets one down in front of me before taking his seat. It smells like heaven, and I can't think of a more comforting meal.

"You cooked the chicken and spaghetti, though? I'm hugely impressed. I burn microwave macaroni and cheese, so anything you do with a burner is already more advanced than my level of cooking."

It's true. You don't want to eat my food for fear of poisoning ... which I actually gave to Presley and me one time when I cooked chicken wings.

"Note to self, never accept an invitation to have you cook for me." He sticks out his tongue, and we both cut into our food.

The first bite is incredible. "I think Carlo's sauce really makes it."

"Hey! I did the heavy lifting, put my heart into it. But ... fine, the sauce is really freaking good."

We lapse into silence for a moment, eating, before Fletcher picks the conversation back up.

"How is the summer course going?"

I take a sip of water to clear my throat. "It's great. The kids are learning a lot. I have them doing these modules I created, of how to stop a minor data breach. Or how to detect what the hacker took using the clues in the code."

"That sounds totally badass. Like some secret spy type of stuff. It always amazes me, what you do. You have to be really smart to understand all of that ... code is like another language."

A small smile stretches my lips. "That's what I always say; I'm fluent in computer. It really is another dialect, and it just happens to come naturally to me. Speaking of that, I got your Etsy page up and running. And I created a brand logo for you, I think you'll like it." I cut into my chicken, fork a piece, and sigh when it hits my tongue.

Fletcher's eyebrows knit together. "You made a logo for me and didn't even run it by me?"

I shrug, not fazed that the move was a tad bossy. "It's not like you bothered having one before. Or a website, or an online storefront. Did you really care what your branding looked like?"

He tips his head to the side, the longer brown locks on the

top of his head shifting to fall over one side of his forehead. "I guess not. I mean, I'd have no idea how to even create branding, much less what I'd want for it. I trust you. Plus, you're hot when you're in charge."

A blush creeps up my neck. He trusts me, that's what he just said. Out of all the men I've been with, not one has uttered that sequence of words to me.

"How is the clock project?"

Fletcher has already finished half his plate, and yet again I'm amazed at how fast men eat. "Going good. The sketches are finalized and have been approved by the town council. So now I just have to start carving, building, working with metal ... which I've never done before. And then there is the whole process of building the mechanism inside. I have no idea how to make a clock actually work ... so it'll take some time."

Just hearing him talk about it, you can see the excitement on his face. "I think it's great, though. You'll get it done. Especially since you're so passionate about it. That's what matters."

"And how about you? Have you found your next passion project?" There is a slight edge to his voice, and I think I know why.

We haven't talked about me staying or going, when it comes to Fawn Hill. This is his home, not mine, and no one in the Nash clan really has any idea how long I'll be in town.

"Not yet. I kind of like teaching the kids, though." I avoid answering in any other real sense, and we finish our meal with small talk about TV shows, sports teams, and the like.

When Fletcher gets up to clear the table, silencing me as I protest that he cooked, I take the time to look around his apartment. It's clean and homey, if not a bit sparse with some outdated pieces. But, he's finally out of his mom's place, and I can thank the privacy gods for that.

"Do you want to go out for ice cream or something? Take a walk in the park?" Fletcher asks as I push out from the table.

Something comes over me, and I realize ... I do not want to do either of those things.

"No. I want you to show me your bedroom."

I don't put on that husky, fake sensual tone that you see in pornos. I also don't wink or raise an eyebrow. I say it to him straight, so that he knows I'm not teasing. I really want him to take me into his room so that we can fall into bed together.

Fletcher must understand that, or maybe he's just taking his reward for putting on an excellent dinner date, because he doesn't hesitate. One second, we're standing a respectable distance apart, and the next, his mouth is covering mine and those sturdy hands are guiding my hips backward toward the bedroom.

We kiss as we stumble toward the mattress, our lips fusing as frustrated breaths slip out. There isn't enough, we seek more as fast as it will come. Another lick, another nip, another tingling sensation that zips down the spine. My need to get out of my clothes and feel him skin to skin is so primal, I find myself growling into his mouth.

Finally, we reach the bed, Fletcher cradling me as we fall, and then adjusting his weight so he doesn't crush me. I writhe under him as we make out, each kiss exploring deeper regions of the other's mouth.

I feel him through his jeans and am again stunned at how huge his penis actually is. Biggest I've ever seen in my life ... and I've been places. Fletcher Nash has a giant cock, no bones about it.

God, it's been months. Too many long months with nothing but my romance novels and vibrator. Even before we broke up, Yanis and I hadn't been having regular sex. I should have known something was off, a Greek god like that brushing me off when I tried to fuck him.

How long had it been, exactly? Six months maybe? Eight? Shit, I was in even more of a dry spell than I'd thought.

It wasn't in my plans to come on to Fletcher tonight. But he cooked this delicious meal, and the music, and he bought me flowers ... and it was the third date.

Shit, I was such a girl. Falling for the easiest tricks in the book. But goddammit, I was too horny to care. And ... I really wanted to know how he'd feel inside me.

"Ryan, wait, let's slow down ..." Even though he says it, Fletcher is still grinding his massive dick against my palm.

I ignore him, trying to free my hands where he's attempting to pin them back against the bed.

"We don't have to—"

"I'm a grown woman, Fletch. It's been months since a man has given me a proper orgasm. I want one. From you. You haven't had sex in five years. Are you really going to stop this?"

His eyes melt into molten blue pools. "That's the second time you've snapped at me while we're pressed together, and I have to say ... it's a big fucking turn on."

"Great. Now put that to good use and screw me sideways," I demand, so amped up on pheromones that I can't see straight.

Fletcher all but shreds the clothes from my body.

In fact, he might actually pop a button or two off the sundress I'm wearing. I borrowed it from Presley, but I'd pay her three times what it cost right now in exchange for Fletcher inside me. I think she'd understand.

"I didn't get to look long enough, last time. My God, you're fucking ..." He trails off, biting down on the fist he shoves into his mouth.

Propping myself up on my elbows and bending a knee, I give him a sexier pose than me just sprawled on the comforter. I know I have a great body, one I work hard for and treat well. I've never been particularly self-conscious, and the fact that Fletcher wants to admire my naked curves ... it turns me on more than it makes me want to hide.

"Well, this isn't fair. Now you've seen me naked twice, and I haven't ever gotten to glimpse that body." I run a finger in the air and then let it drop to my stomach, where I trail it down to the top of my pelvis. It's meant to tease him, but it's also making heat lick up the backs of my thighs in anticipation.

Slowly, he pulls the T-shirt he's wearing over his head, and

I'm treated to a full view of the toned stomach I saw during his run. Not quite weightlifter ripped, Fletcher is fit in a normal way. He's toned, with larger muscles in his lean arms from all the woodworking. The summer months have tanned his skin to a cognac gleam, and that trail of hair I know leads to a sizable cock has me wishing for friction between my legs.

His blue eyes never leave mine as he kicks his shoes off at the same time he unbuckles his belt. All the while I have to keep from putting my hand between my thighs and rubbing. I want him to do that, I've waited so long for him to do that.

With one seamless motion, Fletcher bends down, obscuring himself from view as I try to lift my head higher to see over the edge of his king bed. And then he's back, his long, agile body completely bared to me.

He's gorgeous, all tan skin and dark hair, with the lengthy build of a swimmer. Broad shoulders lead to his trim torso and to narrowed hips. His cock displays itself prominently, not even bobbing in the air, that's how rigid with arousal it is.

I'm about to scoot off the bed and onto my knees, because lord was it an ego boost sucking him off, but Fletcher is too quick for me. In seconds, he's pinning me beneath him, all over our parts lining up in delicious synchronicity.

"I've wanted you like this for a very long time," he whispers, his eyes vulnerable.

I nod. "I've fantasized about you."

He cocks an eyebrow. "I'd like to hear all of those, in vivid detail. But for now, I want to live up to them."

His lips take mine in a haunting, slow perusal. The kiss is gentle but searing, heartfelt but dirty. I have a feeling that everything I assumed about Fletcher Nash in the bedroom is going to be severely shattered in the coming hours.

A callused palm brushes my right nipple, and I gasp into his mouth. He swallows it, never letting up on the kiss as his fingers trace the outline of my breast. Languid digits explore my breasts, hitting all the sensitive spots that make my nerve endings come alive. By the time Fletcher pulls away from my mouth, I'm practically suffocating on my need to come.

With just kisses, he's done that.

His head dips to my left breast, and he plucks my nipple with his teeth. I can't stop watching him as he explores my body; it's like I'm participating, but I'm not. I'm a voyeur, getting turned on simply from the act of watching him turn me on.

After a few minutes, he picks his head up and looks me in the eyes.

"I'm not sure how long I'll last. So, I'm going to make you come with my mouth first. Your taste on my tongue, that's what I want to remember far after this is over."

Those words alone have me dripping wet arousal onto the sheets.

With that, Fletcher's face disappears between my legs, and in another instant, I'm throwing my head back into the mattress.

"Oh, fuck, yes ..." I moan loudly, because it's been too long since a man's mouth was where I desperately need it to be.

I've always loved sex. Everything about it, from the dirty to the intimate. It's natural for me to crave foreplay and intercourse all hours of the day. The fact that I wasn't feeding that need, especially with Fletcher, is a damn shame. One we'll have to make up for over and over again tonight.

Especially, since this man knows what he's doing with this mouth. He licks up my center, his tongue flat and wide, until I'm oversensitive and writhing. My fists dig into the sheets, and I want to grip his hair and grind down onto his face, but I can't seem to move my rubbery muscles. That's when Fletcher blows lightly on my clit, and I nearly catapult to the ceiling. But he doesn't let up, following that up with a nip of his teeth on the bundle of nerves, and immediately inserting one digit between my swollen lips.

"Gahhh ..." The sounds I'm making aren't even intelligible.

Fletcher pumps me, adding another finger as I begin to almost yell. I can feel it building, the orgasm swirling like a devastating tornado low inside my core. And when he scrapes his teeth against my clit once more, I'm swept up, flying through the air with no care as to how I land.

I'm coming in breathy shudders and am acutely aware that Fletcher sits back on his haunches to watch me unravel. His eyes could make me come again, that's how predatory they are.

"I want you inside me." The whisper comes out as the wracks from my orgasm begin to leave my body.

"Let me get a condom." He's about to hop out of the bed when I put a hand on his arm.

"You don't need one." The imperceptible shake of my head has his eyes going wide.

My statement says that I trust him. That I know he's safe, and so am I.

With the hand on his arm, I pull him toward me, until we're lined up exactly how we were made to be. He fits me, and I fit him.

"I haven't done this in a long time ..." Those blue eyes are already trying to apologize, and he isn't even in me.

"I want to watch you come," I say, giving him full consent to focus only on himself when his cock enters me.

Fletcher took care of me. Now, I want to take care of him.

Slowly, he pushes inside. His cock is so big, it takes three tries of pulling out and rubbing the wetness around my lips to get enough lubrication for him to slide in. When he does, I have to suck in, because it's a been a while and he's the largest man I've ever slept with.

"Am I hurting you?" His eyebrows are pinched together in

harsh concentration, and I can see the veins popping out on his neck.

He's trying so hard to stay in control, so hard to not let his climax take over.

"In the best way possible." I let out a breathy laugh as I wiggle my hips, adjusting until I'm comfortable.

Once he's seated all the way to his balls, I pull his hips into me, showing him it's okay.

"*Fuck*." Fletcher drops his forehead to mine, scrunching his eyes closed. "I'm not going to last much longer."

Nipping at his earlobe, I whisper into it. "Let go."

And he does. In three long, hard, powerful strokes, Fletcher is growling and cursing the heavens as I feel him release inside me. His face is wild, pained, relieved … but most of all, free.

It's a beautiful thing to watch, seeing someone with his control and restrictions be completely unconfined.

Fletcher collapses onto me, stroking my hair while he's still lodged firmly inside me.

"Thank you," he says, and I know it's not in a cheesy way.

He means it. I helped him move past something that has been holding him back. And in a way, he has done the same for me.

Suddenly, I'm so tired, I can't even stand. I must begin to doze, because I'm aware of Fletcher pulling the sheets over us.

Before I nod off, I wonder if it wouldn't be so crazy if we decided to take care of each other, permanently.

"**G**et ready to give us your money, boys."

Penelope rattles the chips in her hand, and Forrest rolls his eyes.

"You don't even know how to play poker. I heard you asking Travis to help you google the rules before." My brother can't help but get competitive with his wife.

"It's okay, I'm going to lose anyway. I have no idea how to play this." Lily giggles. "I just came for the night off and the free lemonade."

As usual, our poker night was alcohol-free. But something it included tonight that it didn't normally? The Nash women.

And Ryan, of course. The two of us can't stop eyeing each other across the table in Keaton's basement.

"Don't worry, Lil. I'm not that good, either." Ryan pops a pretzel in her mouth, and I think about what she looks like when she comes.

It's been two days since she left my apartment the morning after I cooked her dinner, and I can think of little else than my reintroduction to sex. Or, more accurately, who introduced me. If I had known Ryan Shea was going to be so downright fucking sexy in bed, I would have given up the whole celibacy schtick years ago.

Maybe I had known, and that's why I avoided her for so long. Either way, I could barely contain myself from dragging her out of here over my shoulder to go another three rounds.

When Presley insisted on an all-family poker night, we guys had groaned about it. This was our thing, our time as brothers. We talked shit, didn't have women nagging us, and could burp as much as we wanted.

But now that all four women were present, I was happy as a pig in shit. It gave me ample opportunity to make flirty eyes at Ryan.

I've never slept with another person in my bed while I was sober. In my heyday of drunkenness, I'd wake up on coffee tables, crammed into couches, in the back of a pickup truck that wasn't mine. Sometimes there would be a girl under my arm, sometimes there would be a whole slew of people next to me. I'd never know what had happened the night before.

But when I woke up to Ryan in my bed, her warm, naked body there for me to wrap my arms around and pull in ... it was one of the most indescribable feelings in the world. It hit me; maybe this is why my brothers are so gaga over their women. Because they get *this* every day. Just holding her was incredible enough, but then she'd stirred from her sleep and drowsily laid her lips on mine before straddling my hardening cock and riding me in a daze of dreams and sunrise.

Christ ... I was getting a boner just thinking about it.

I cover my lap as Bowen and Presley finally take their seats around the table, snacks in hand.

"All right, we're playing stud poker, which means everyone is dealt five cards, and will try to work out the best hand they can from those. We'll go around, placing bets, until someone folds because they're a little bitch who can't stand the heat." Forrest describes the game in a crude manner, and Bowen rolls his eyes.

"Or because they can't count, like me." I lighten the mood with a little self-deprecation, if nothing else than to make the women feel better.

"If you have a question, don't ask it. Loser has to jump in the lake in Bloomfield Park, naked." Forrest finishes his lightning round of rules with a hand wave and then begins to deal.

"No, they don't!" Lily protests, looking to Bowen for backup.

"I'll take your loss if you lose." Ryan leans over and rubs a hand over Lily's arms. "I could use the dip anyway. It's humid as hell here."

And now I was definitely going to lose the poker game because I couldn't stop picturing Ryan's perfect tits and round, smooth ass dripping with lake water.

Everyone gets their cards, and the looks being exchanged around the table are comical. My brothers are eyeing their wives up, and the girls are trying to throw these tough expressions out there like that will help them win the game.

"Gah, I fold." Lily immediately puts her cards down. "Y'all know I'm not a good liar."

"Babe! You didn't even let me see your hand to know if you had a good one!" Bowen laughs but then gives his wife a kiss on the forehead.

"So, who is going to quit while they're ahead? Or, just give me all your money. You know you want to," Forrest taunts.

Keaton throws in a one-dollar chip, while Forrest and Bowen throw in fivers, and Presley and Penelope match them. I put in a twenty-five-dollar chip, feeling pretty confident about my full house, and when it comes around to Ryan, she throws in a black hundred-dollar coin.

We're not really playing for that much money, but we use the chips that came with the poker set Keaton bought. The highest we'll go is a ten-dollar bet, which is what she just threw in.

Bowen snickers. "You sure about that?"

Ryan shrugs. "I just like the color black."

We go around again, placing bets and trying to pull off our best poker faces. At the end of the first hand, it's down to Ryan, Forrest, and me, with a sizable pot in the middle of the table.

"Lay down your guns, Ry. You don't want this to get ugly," Forrest tells her.

She's either got a hell of a hand or has no idea what she's doing. Either way, if my twin is throwing out black chips the way he is, he must have some good cards.

"I'm out." I fold my cards and throw them down, not really caring that I just lost my "money."

"All right, I'm all in." Forrest winks a cocky eye at Ryan.

Her jet-black hair moves slightly around her shoulders as she cocks her head to the side. It catches the light and shines like a dark diamond in my direction, and I'm momentarily distracted.

"I'll go all in, too." She nods, and I can't tell if she's playing right into his hands or playing *him*.

Forrest looks like someone peed in his Cheerios but flourishes his cards on the table. "Four of a kind. Now give me my money."

He begins to reach toward the middle of the table, but a *tsk* of Ryan's tongue has him pausing, and all of us looking toward her.

"Straight flush. I think I won, didn't I?"

The words come out of her mouth like she knew what she was doing this whole time and was playing us all with her dumb girl routine.

"She's a goddamn hustler!" Forrest cries as Ryan rakes everyone's chips across the table, smiling a devilish little grin.

Presley snickers. "Did I forget to mention that Ryan played in some pretty prominent amateur poker tournaments?"

Keaton raises an eyebrow at his wife. "Why yes, you did conveniently forget to mention that."

"You're a dirty little cheat." The smile I give Ryan is so wide, I think I'm about to start cackling.

This woman continues to surprise me, in the best ways possible. Smart as a whip, sexy as hell, a knockout in bed, and she knows how to run a poker table? Should I just get down on one knee now?

"The biggest mistake is underestimating one's opponent on the table. If you don't know what they're capable of, how can you ever see them coming?" She winks at me, and I want to pin her hands above her head and torture her slowly with my mouth.

"So, who has to skinny dip in the lake now that Ms. Poker over here has shown her true ability?" Presley folds her arms across her chest, eyeing Keaton up like he's her next meal.

He holds his hands up. "You know I only get undressed for you, babe."

We all crack up, because it's so unlike my big brother to say something like that.

She's right, though. In the sense that, if you didn't know what a person was capable of, you'd never see them coming until they hit you full force. Kind of like she had with me. I hadn't bothered to know Ryan Shea, because I was too damned scared and selfish focusing on my own struggle.

But the minute I opened myself up to the idea of her, she slammed into me like a freight train. And now I couldn't escape the way everything about her was slowly taking over my brain.

Nor did I want to.

26

I've just stepped out of the shower when my phone rings.

Glancing at the clock on the nightstand, it reads 4:30 p.m., and I realize I only have an hour before Fletcher comes over with dinner after his shift.

He's supposed to be bringing lemon pepper chicken wings and a few other specialties from Kip's Diner, things I haven't tried yet and he's appalled I haven't sampled. But at the rate I'm going, my hair will still be wet when he arrives.

Not that I ever make much of an effort with my daily appearance. A quick blow dry, a swipe of mascara, a spritz of perfume. I'm gifted with high cheekbones and pretty manageable natural hair, which I thank my lucky stars for.

I'm scared to look at the screen of my cell, because I know who's calling. Yanis stopped contacting me months ago ... and I'm surprised in this moment that I haven't thought of him in that long, too. Maybe Presley was right when she said I felt differently about certain men. Or maybe it was because I had a new man on my mind ... that was typically how I operated.

How could I tell if I really felt differently about Fletcher, or if

I was just using this relationship with its shiny new sex presents as a distraction?

Shaking that unwanted thought from my brain, I pick it up to see my mom's name flashing across the screen.

My sigh is audible in the small guest cottage, and I wish someone was here to swat the damn thing out of my grip. Her calls have been increasing, and this is the fourth one in the many months I've taken up residence in Fawn Hill. Four calls in a couple months might not sound like a lot, but after not hearing from someone in a year and a half, it was odd. And since this is my junkie mother we're talking about, it is dangerously suspicious.

I didn't want to hear her voice. I didn't want my heart to weep for the mother she should have been, or for the childhood I could have had. I didn't want to worry about her, because I shouldn't have to. And I didn't want to have to refuse, essentially sentencing her to mania, when she asked me for money to get high.

So, instead of taking the call, like I've done so many times before, I send it to voicemail.

And in a moment of spontaneous growth and courage, my finger hits the block button before I can think about stopping it. Time seems to stop for a nanosecond, and I hold my breath, expecting the sky to fall or something equally as disastrously grand.

But nothing does.

Life just keeps on going. I get a Facebook notification from a friend in Germany, somewhere down the block a neighbor is cutting their lawn. I know when I walk out of the cottage door, sunshine and humidity will greet me. I'll go teach the kids in my summer course tomorrow, and I'll still be able to grab drinks with the girls on Friday night.

For so long, I allowed this idea of my mother to fill my soul with tension and dread. Would I get a phone that she over-dosed? Would she show up at my job asking for money? Would my life suffer if I cut her out completely ... because after all, she's the only blood relative I know of. It seemed like a harsh mistake to end our relationship, because I was the child and love from my mother was something that was supposed to be a no brainer. It was simply supposed to exist.

But it didn't have to be like that. The families we were born into didn't have to be that source of love for us. We could find it in other ways, like the friendship I had with Presley. Recognizing that some bonds were toxic ... it was a relief.

That's what I had just done, the minute I'd stopped making it possible for her to contact me.

I rub a fist into my chest and sit down on the edge of the bed, thinking there should be some monumental swell of emotions in me. And maybe relief is there, but sadness and hurt ... I think they left a long time ago where my mother is concerned.

My stomach grumbles, and I have to laugh, because if this isn't my body's way of telling me that life goes on, I don't know what is.

Realizing I can't wait another hour for food, I throw on the outfit I'd already picked for when Fletcher arrives and make my way through the backyard and into Presley's kitchen. I find Hattie sitting at the kitchen counter.

"Hey," I say warmly, giving her a side hug before moving to explore the pantry.

"Hiya," she responds, popping a piece of watermelon in her mouth. "The course going well?"

It's what she asks me every time I see her. I'm not sure if she really just wants to know that, but I suspect the question is deeper. Part of me suspects Hattie wants me to plant permanent *roots* in Fawn Hill, and that's just her way of planting the seed in my *head*.

She isn't the only one who's tried to broach the subject. Presley slips it into conversation now and then, Lily told me the other day that she thinks it would be so sweet if I moved to town, and then there was the whole awkward encounter with Fletcher at his kitchen table.

The truth is ... I don't see myself staying in this small town for the rest of my life. Sure, I like it well enough, and this break was long overdue. But I'm a traveler; wanderlust has infected me like a virus, and the only cure is to take off for the next destination. I like having a home base to come back to, and maybe Fawn Hill could be that, but I wouldn't be me if I didn't spend a month in Vienna and the next in Bermuda.

Ducking into the fridge, I grab a snack pack of pretzels and cream cheese. Keaton buys them for himself, but I've become addicted, and subsequently stolen his supply over the last month.

Opening it and popping the first dunked pretzel in my mouth, I nod. "The kids are really getting the hang of it. I should have thanked you a while ago, I'm so—"

"Don't you go apologizing now. There is no need. I just brought two things together that we're looking for each other. That's thanks enough for me. It suits you, teaching. You should think about doing it long term."

And there it is, that little suggestion again. I'm not one for running at the first sign of commitment, that was never my problem. No, Presley and I used to joke that she ran to avoid getting hurt by anyone, and I ran only after I'd been hurt and overstayed my welcome. Was that what I was doing here?

"What? Do I have 'I'm in my thirties and still don't know where my life is going' stamped on my forehead?" I joke, only half meaning it.

Hattie raises her eyebrows at me. "I'm not the one who said it. But if you think about it, you do know where you're going. You know a lot more about yourself than most. You're just scared to implement the decisions you know those preferences call for."

"Like what?" I ask, genuinely curious now.

"You know you love computers, but you're tired of your job. Perhaps you've outgrown it, or more likely, you need a position that calls for more than just fixing rich people's problems. What you crave is to help those who could really do good with the skills you can teach. And in doing so, you do good yourself."

Jeez, I wasn't looking for a therapy session when I came in here, but Hattie is taking me to church.

When I don't reply, she goes on. "The need for comfort and security constantly battles your desire to see the world. You can have both, you know. A hometown and adventures abroad. You've done it before, but maybe it's time to establish a new place to store your clothes. The same goes for love. You've done it before, but this time, with that strapping youngest Nash boy, it's different. We all see it. I don't even have to know your dating history to know that the way you look at each other, it's the real deal."

How the hell could she possibly know all of this? It's like she's reading my mind, and I can't stop her. In a very short amount of time, I've come to care deeply for Fletcher. Not just on a romantic level, but I respect his drive and his values. I don't think I can say that for any of my past relationships ... those were all just fluff compared with the things I see in Fletcher.

"And last, your biological mother. I'm not even going to sugar-coat this one. It is far past time to cut her out of your life. She's toxic, she's cancer, and she's eating up the confidence and good self-worth you have with each time she dials your num—"

This one, I can give her an answer to, so I cut her off.

"I've stopped taking her phone calls, and ... I just blocked her number." I breathe, because just saying it feels like a huge weight off of me.

Hattie's expression turns from one of sternness, to surprise. "Well ... good. No one like that deserves your love or attention. And if you ever need an ear to listen, I'm here. We're your family, have been since the day Presley told me about her wacky new roommate in New York."

"Aren't you just supposed to say some mumbo jumbo about following my destiny, or seeing the light? From what I hear, you never give Presley the answers, you just guide her in the right direction. Why spell it all out for me?"

Hattie's smile is small. "Because *you* already know the answers. You're just sitting on your ass, pretending that you don't. With Presley, she really didn't know what she wanted out of life. You, Ryan, have all the options listed in front of you, but you simply won't choose. That's why. It's time to make your choice."

"Just because you say so?" Her words mildly annoy me, but the beat of my heart tells me she's dangerously close to having my number.

Hattie rises, patting me on the shoulder. "I'm an old woman, close to death. I don't mince words anymore, and you should take my advice before I'm gone."

I yell after her, "You can't play that card! It won't work with me, Presley has warned me!"

The chuckle I hear down the hall tells me she doesn't believe me. And to be honest, I don't believe myself either.

"Y**ou do know that camping is literally the worst thing you could force me to do, right?"

Inspecting the nature around us, I screw up my face and stick out my tongue.

"Oh, come on, it's not so bad. You've hiked in Hawaii before, and you liked those hot springs in Iceland." Presley tries to point these adventures out as if they're anything like sleeping in a sweat cocoon on a floor of dirt.

"Those were beautiful, enchanting vacation experiences. I'd rather stick a fork in my eyeball than pee in a bucket and roast trout over a fire we started ourselves."

Okay, I know I sound like a brat ... but I'm a city girl. Fawn Hill is about as country as it gets for me, and then the Nash family decided to take me even further past my limits.

"I know whose sleeping bag I'm leaving a dead spider in," Travis whispers loudly behind his hand to his little brothers, and I shoot him a death glare.

The whole crew decided to come along on this jaunt into the forest, with Penelope and Forrest bringing the kids. The only person not here is Lily, who opted to stay home with the baby.

But since Bowen is the most rugged of all the brothers, and the one who knows the most about camping, he's here to make sure we don't kill ourselves.

Now that Fletcher and I have spent the last week and a half sleeping in each other's beds, it seems the cat's out of the bag. The group already assumes we'll be sharing a tent, so when shelter setup starts, Presley just throws me a nod and tells me to get to work on my love shack.

One look at the man I've been sharing a mattress with, and I know we'll have to zipper that tent door tight and keep the noise down. Damn, does he look *fine*. He's got about three days' worth of stubble on his jaw, a red flannel shirt open and flapping in the breeze, with nothing beneath it but bare skin, and hiking boots that make me want to drag him into the woods. He's like a sexy lumberjack on a stick, and that's usually not my type, but hell, if he isn't *doing it* for me today.

Really, he does it for me every day. We've been practically inseparable the last two weeks, and the ways in which we've gotten to know each other ...

My cheeks heat wildly just at the thought. It's more than that, though. Fletcher and I spend hours talking; we discuss his goals, my travels, his family, what we like most in the world and what we hate. The connection is deep, infusing itself in my marrow. In the past, I've been swept along the current of lust for the man I'm with. But with him ... it's the complete package.

That scares me more than I'm ready to admit.

"Ready to set up our Hotel de Dirt?" I joke to him as I unbuckle some part of the tent material that I'm pretty sure I wasn't supposed to touch.

"Sure," he deadpans, his face blank.

Fletcher has seemed off all day. He's cold, aloof, has barely cracked a joke, which is so unlike him ... and he was snippy to the kids while unloading the car. I've never seen him do that, and that's how I know something is really wrong.

"Are you okay?" I ask in a low voice, so no one can hear me.

"I'm fine." His voice is a hard clip.

I'm beginning to get ticked off, because I'm not an idiot. "Clearly, you're not. Do you want to talk about it?"

Fletcher shoots an angry huff in my direction. "No. Just drop it."

That pisses me off even more. I don't care about a lot of people, but I care about him. And the way he's brushing me off when I'm only trying to help? That makes me angry, but I swallow it. He needs compassion more than he needs my ire.

I go to him, resting a hand on his bicep. "Fletcher, what is it? Let me help you."

"I ... never mind. You won't understand." He wrenches out of my hold, rather harshly, and stomps away.

Presley looks at me quizzically, but tosses her head in Fletcher's retreating direction, and I nod, letting her know I'm going after him.

He's moving at such a fast pace, I have to jog to keep up. By the time I look up, we're a distance away from the campsite.

We're far enough into the trees now that the others wouldn't be able to hear us if I yelled for them, not that I'll need to. Fletcher's in a bad mood, not dangerous.

"Fletch, I'm asking you to talk to me. Don't pull this bullshit. We've never done the dramatics with one and other, let's not start now." Maybe he'll listen to reason.

His forward progress halts, but he still gives me his flannel-clad back. Those big, capable hands come up to rake through his hair, and I can feel the frustration rolling off him in waves.

When he speaks, his voice is a hoarse, pained thing. "I ... have days. It's been years since I got sober, so they're few and far between, but they still happen. I'll go through an entire week, never thinking once about being an alcoholic. And then, it's like a switch flips. I'll wake up one morning, like today, and the need to drink burns so badly in my throat that I have to physically hurt myself in order to not ravage the town in search of alcohol."

My gaze falls to his bruised, scabbing knuckles, and I'm surprised I didn't see them before.

"What can I do to help?" I ask, genuinely trying to ease his agony.

The look he gives me is one of utter disdain. "Nothing, Ryan. You can't do a thing. Isn't this what you're afraid of? What everyone's afraid of? That I'll drink myself back into oblivion? I don't even understand why you're with me. Just ... get away from me."

He's angry and deflecting, and I should get away from him. But I understand him too much, in a way he doesn't even realize.

"Take it out on me. You have a craving? Use my body to satisfy it." My words might sound shaky, but I'm puffing out my chest like I'm not scared of a thing he could do to me.

I'm not scared of him, he's Fletcher. But right now? He's looking at me as if he could rip me in two and not bat an eye about it. I haven't encountered this Fletcher yet, the restless addict in need of a hit.

That expression that he might tear me down, disappear on me, fail completely in his sobriety ... or all three at once. That's what I'm afraid of when it comes to him. Except I know, just like I do with my mother, that he needs to lean on me. And despite all the warning signs I've taught myself, I'm in too deep when it comes to my feelings for Fletcher. I'm half in love with the man.

So instead, I'll sacrifice myself to this side of him in hopes I'll get the wonderful side back.

He comes crashing into me, my back hitting hard against a rough tree just behind me. Fletcher's bruised and bloody knuckles catch my skull before it hits, and then he's consuming me. Biting at my lips, kissing them so aggressively that I know he'll leave a mark.

Rough fingertips pull at my T-shirt and shorts, trying to shove it all aside. I can't think straight, the rough pleasure he's delivering in the form of his whiskery mouth to my neck has my knees buckling. My hands go to his open shirt, tracing the muscles of his abdomen in hurried circles.

"Turn around," he growls, half moving even though he commanded what I should do.

Pressed up against the tree, the bark digging into my palms, I'm panting like a wanton animal, exposing myself for Fletcher to do as he pleases.

Behind me, I hear the pull of his zipper, the ragged breaths that burst from his lungs. And then my shorts are pulled quickly down my legs, coming to rest at my ankles, above my shoes. Fletcher does the same with my thong, pulling it just far enough so that he can enter me unhindered by the scrap of lace.

My skin crawls with goose bumps as he slides an arm around my waist, holding me flush against him. The other arm comes under my right arm and across my chest. Fletcher has a full hold on me, and I'm not going anywhere.

"If you have to yell, bite into my arm." He growls and then slams into me.

I'm so shocked, my voice doesn't even work to do that. The sensation of him invading me, the sting of it accompanied by the wetness that started pooling the minute I heard the hiss of his zipper ... it's unlike any other arousal I've felt before. Fletcher is possessive in a way that's not being put on; this isn't just some role play fantasy or kinky shit.

This is raw. His need is so heightened, he might leave fingerprint-sized bruises on my hip. Knowing that I can be his cure ... it's intoxicating.

Fletcher pumps me, never letting up, each of us biting our

lips and each other's arms or necks to stop from howling like wild animals. This is fucking ... blind, primal fucking. It's needing the surrender of someone else's body for your pleasure.

My orgasm doesn't sneak up on me, it isn't a slow build to a cascading waterfall of release. No, it's a seven-forty-seven to the gut, slamming into me like a plane crash landing and exploding on impact.

I start to scream as it crushes my organs in its wake, pleasure radiating from every cell, when Fletcher slaps a hand over my mouth. He fucks me like this, savagely, drawing my hips down onto him with one arm and silencing me with the other.

"You save me. Only you, Ryan ... only ... you ..."

Fletcher breaks off in a shuddering groan, burying his face in my hair so that it muffles the dull roar he lets out. His hips jut up into me, his cock pulsing as he releases all the pent up cravings into me.

"I can't let you go, now. You're in me, right here." He moves my hand to chest, splaying it directly where his heart beats. "Please, don't make me."

For the first time in my life, a man is telling me that it's my choice whether or not to break us. Fletcher's declaration is more than love, it's complete surrender. Of his heart, to me. He's handing it over, telling me that I'm responsible for keeping us whole, and not the other way around.

I've waited a lifetime for someone to give me a gift like this. But now that he has, I'm not sure I can bear the weight of it.

B y the time we straighten our clothes and head back for the campsite, the intense craving that had been building in my chest since I woke up has completely left my body.

In its wake though, it's left a blackhole-sized wreckage that plagues me with every step.

What the fuck did I say to Ryan? Why the fuck did I have to go and spill my guts on her like that?

She's walking ahead of me, as I instructed her to, because we're wading through brush and branches in a thicket of forest, and all I want to do is stop her and take it all back. Is she freaked out? Probably, considering I told her when we started this that we were going to take things slow and had no pressure on us.

What a fucking moron I am. I all but told the woman I loved her after like a month of dating.

Not that it isn't true, but she didn't need to hear all that. The whole point of convincing Ryan to date me was to prove to her I'm not like the guys of her past; I wanted to get to know her and not move hot and heavy until we burned out like a shooting star.

Now I've ruined it, because post-coital feelings grabbed me by my emptied balls and had me confessing true love.

"I'm, uh, going to grab a shower down at the bathhouse." Ryan's eyes don't even come close to holding mine as we walk back into camp.

"Where have you two been?" My twin brother waggles his eyebrows at me.

We ignore him as I head to set up our discarded tent, and Ryan grabs her bag to head for the bathrooms.

"You okay?" I hear Presley ask when her friend passes, and I look to see Ryan nod and then walk off.

I should have distanced myself ... I thought as much before asking her to come on this camping trip with my family. We've been attached at the hip for two weeks, and if I'm not working or in my shop on the farm, I'm with Ryan. We eat almost every meal together, spend hours in each other's beds, and she's gotten into the habit of walking to the grocery store to meet me and walk home after my shift.

I realized I was in love with her about five days ago when she laid two slices of almost burned bacon on my plate. Not because she was a bad cook—she claimed to be, but I found out she just didn't like it—or because she liked them that way, but because I did. She'd cooked, an activity she despised, for me and made my breakfast food exactly how I liked it. It was so simple ... but to me, it was a grand gesture.

At that moment, I'd looked up into her sleepy morning smile, smelling that fruity Chapstick she was always wearing ... and I knew. I am in love with Ryan Shea.

I probably had been on the cusp of it for a while before that ... maybe even from the moment I met her. I didn't put much stock into love at first sight, but knowing how I felt about her now, I should have.

After I set up our tent, I move the rest of our bags inside, unroll the sleeping bags and throw a pillow at the top of each one. We're ready to sleep on the ground for the night, although I know Ryan is less than pleased about the arrangements.

It's about half an hour before she comes back into the campsite, and she's changed from jean shorts and a T-shirt into black yoga pants and a long black tank top. The ensemble matches her hair, and when she ducks inside the tent and comes back out, there is a big wool sweater engulfing her body.

I didn't realize how chilly it would get out here, it's been a while since I've gone camping. Apparently, the city girl is more prepared than I am.

Over the course of the next two hours, we all help cook dinner, eat, clean up, and then start a fire in the common area we've made with our tents. My nephews are sword fighting with large sticks they found in the woods, Presley and Keaton are uncharacteristically showing a lot of PDA, and Bowen is Face-Timing with Lily and the baby. Penelope is busy setting up s'mores supplies, and my twin brother is probably taking a rest in his tent.

But Ryan is right here next to me, and I know we need to talk.

"Hey, do you want to—" I begin, but my sister-in-law cuts me off.

"S'mores, y'all! Come and gather round!" Penelope claps her hands cheerfully, and I think she might be more excited about the bonding than the sugar we're about to consume.

Me? I could use some chocolate therapy. Sugar to an addict is the next best thing to getting drunk or high. That and cigarettes, but I never much got the taste for them.

Everyone jokes around at first, seeing who can light their marshmallow on fire or toast it perfectly. Ames accidentally drops his entire stick in the fire, and we all rag on him for his burned treat smoldering in the fire.

"What is the thing you fear most?" Presley starts in a spooky growl, like she's a camp counselor trying to start a scary story circle.

The campfire flickers and illuminates everyone's faces, and Bowen, who she turns to first since he's sitting right next to her, ignores the question to make his fourth s'more.

"Snakes! I really hate snakes." Matthew nods gravely, and Forrest shoots his stepson a fist bump, as if to say he, too, is scared of snakes.

"Laundry. I fear laundry. Especially stinky, smelly, little boy laundry." Penelope bends her arms at the elbows and presses her palms to her cheeks, as if she's quaking in her boots.

The boys crack up, booing their mom for making fun of them.

"Well, I was always especially afraid of under the bed. Even now, I can't sleep with one foot out of the comforter, or I think some monster will reach up and grab it." Ryan shivers as if she's thinking about it.

"How about you, Fletch? You know, he used to be terrified of Daffy Duck." Keaton laughs as if just remembering the memory.

I've been lost in my own thoughts, half-listening while staring into the fire, but I glance up at the sound of my name. This is a fun, family bonding time, but I'd be lying if I told them anything other than the one thing I fear the most.

Falling off the wagon.

My biggest fear is getting my hands on a bottle and never letting go. Is that what they want to hear, though? Hell, no.

"Yeah, he was pretty scary with that voice." I laugh along, but my heart isn't in it.

I feel Ryan's eyes on me as the group moves on to the next question, or some kiddish form of truth or dare. Honestly, I'm not really paying attention.

"Do you want to call it a night?" Ryan asks, as if reading my mind.

"Yeah, I'm pretty tired," I tell her, glad for the excuse to get up and tell everyone good night.

We walk to our tent, not touching each other, and I feel like the biggest jackass in the world. For the words I should have held back, for attacking her like a savage, for letting her see my true struggle with sobriety.

Ryan turns away when we crawl through the zippered opening, and as I close it, I see her beginning to undress and slip into her warm pajamas.

"Hey, so ..." My voice is awkward, and the woman I care about very deeply feels a million miles away.

"I'm pretty tired. Let's just ... sleep." She tosses a look over her shoulder that says she can't do this right now.

I've never seen her whiskey-colored eyes so guarded, not even when we were trying to deny that there was any spark between us.

Nodding, I set to throwing on my fleece-lined sleeping gear. Earlier, I thought we'd unzip both sleeping bags and lay on one while the other was thrown over us, giving us unfettered access to ... keep each other warm, if you know what I mean. But Ryan just tucks herself into the singular sleeping bag, and I can't help the disappointment that pings my heart.

Once I fold my body into my own, I flip the switch on the battery-operated lamp beside me, and we're plunged into darkness. I can hear my family still outside around the fire, laughing and talking about whatever topic they're onto now.

Ryan flips over with a huff, and apparently, we're not just going to drift off into awkward sleep. "What you said earlier ..."

"Ryan, you don't have to ... we don't have to talk about it. I didn't mean it." I try to take the coward's way out.

"Yes, you did, don't play that bullshit with me," she snaps, and I know I've hurt her.

Scooting to close the space, I pull her into my arms, our sleeping bags bunching between us. Even in the few hours she's been distant, I've missed her being here. "I'm sorry. You're right. I did mean it. But, it doesn't mean you have to talk about it."

Ryan blinks slowly, her chin tipped up to look me in the eyes. "I know I don't. It scares me. We were ... taking things slow, and you had to go and say all of that."

I press a kiss to her forehead, because I can't not breathe her in. This thread between us feels finite, in this moment, like anything could snap it. I long for her, yearn to do this for a long time to come. Does her being scared of that mean ... she doesn't want it, too? Either way, I have to own my feelings now. They're out there, and I've held myself back from what I wanted for a very long time. It's within arm's reach, and I'd be an idiot to let it go now.

"I know I said that we could just ... hang out. But, come on, Ryan. I think we both knew from the moment we said that, that it wouldn't be true. It might seem fast, or too much this early in the grand scheme of whatever we're doing together, but I don't care anymore. I've felt something for you since the moment you walked into that rehearsal dinner for Presley and Keaton. You infected me, you got straight down into my marrow. The instant buzz that started between us, it's a once in a blue moon thing. I've never felt the way I feel about you about anyone, that's just a fact. You're the first person I think about when I wake up, and you pop into my head a million times a day. When I'm with you, I forget about all the bad shit I've done, I forget the doubt that tells me I'll never be the man I'm trying to be. Because for you, I want to be him. So yes, I want you to stay with me. I don't ever want to let you go."

"I'm scared," she says it again. The only two words in response to my quiet declaration in the darkness of our tent.

"Why?" My voice is a whisper.

"Because I feel it, too."

Her short confirmation is all I need, a big, verbose confession to match mine isn't necessary.

Without wasting another second, I kick out of my sleeping bag and make for hers, unzipping the side and making her giggle as I struggle to climb in next to her.

She stops laughing, though, when I cover her mouth in a gentle, deep, endless kiss.

We make love in slow, tender strokes, using the other's mouth to silence the sounds from carrying past the paper-thin tent walls.

The summer ends in a flurry of squirreling away days in the sun, after-dinner ice cream trips and hoarding every possible second I can spend with Ryan.

September rushes by as well, the kids go back to school; I bury myself in the clock tower project, and Ryan gets hired as a computer aide in the middle school. The job is temporary, and it makes me wonder if that means she is as well, but I don't push the issue.

We're all but living together, with her going back to the guest cottage every few days for clean underwear. And ... it's settled into a nice routine. She teaches three days a week, while I work my day job. I was promoted to manager at the grocery store and had a few more projects come in, so I can afford to take her out on the weekends. Probably nowhere near as fancy as she's used to in New York, but she never says anything.

Anyway, I cook us dinner, Ryan got me into bingeing *Game of Thrones* ... even though I lie to Forrest and still tell him I'd never watch that nerd show. On the weekends, we hang out with my family or I take her to some of my favorite secluded spots in the county. For claiming she hates nature, she sure does love the hidden gems I show her.

All in all, we've settled into my idea of the perfect relationship. I get to spend all my free time with her, and the sex is still off the charts.

And then, October rolls around, and I wake up into my own personal day of hell.

From the start of this Wednesday morning, Ryan knows something's up. I barely get out of bed, and I didn't tell her that I requested off of work a week ago specifically so I could mope around.

"Hey, get up, you're going to be late." She pulls on a pair of yoga leggings, preparing to go take Presley's morning class.

"I'm not going." I know I sound like a petulant child, but I can't help it.

Grief will do that to you, make you an irrational son of a bitch. The days I wake up and feel the need for a drink burn so harshly in my throat that it's a like a wildfire rushed through there ... those are hard days.

But those days are nothing compared to this day.

"Do you feel sick?" Now her attention is fully on me, my gorgeous girlfriend standing at the foot of the bed staring at me.

Her eyes hold sympathy, but also suspicion. I've never done this before, even on a day where I feel like my sobriety is slipping, and Ryan looks worried.

"No, I just ... go to your class. I'm going to stay in bed." I flip over, burying my head between the pillows.

My heart weighs about a thousand pounds in my chest, and even if I wanted to, I have no energy to leave the mattress.

Ryan sits down beside me, her body making the bed dip, and rubs a hand up and down my back. "I'm not going to class while you're like this. Talk to me, Fletch."

For someone who appears so callous and off-limits in her

city-girl attitude, Ryan is extremely caring and kind. It's something I've come to learn over the last two months while we've spent all this time together. There is no one more ready and willing to listen than this woman.

Too bad I feel like wallowing in my sadness. "Go, Ryan. I need some time."

And even though she's empathetic, Ryan also knows when to walk away. She isn't a woman who will let you treat her like crap because you feel like crap. She told me as much when we were talking about her past relationships one night. It's something she's trying to change, and even if I'm gloomy right now, I respect it when she gets up, tells me she'll be home in an hour, and walks out the door.

Once she's gone, I flip over onto my back and inspect the ceiling.

Eight years ago today, my father died.

It's a weird thing to think, that he's been gone for almost a decade. I spent so much of my life with him, but sooner than I realize, I'll have spent just as much time with him gone. The thought makes me want to rage, to punch holes in the wall or fuck up my life worse than I have in the past. If it wasn't for the debilitating sorrow keeping me chained beneath the sheets, I probably would.

I drift in and out of a hazy, restless sleep as I wonder what Dad would say if he were here today. Would he approve of Ryan? Hell, he'd probably like her more than he liked me. Would he be proud that my creation was going to be displayed up there in that clock tower? Would he rag on me for renting a place above Carlucci's, or use it to score more free pizza? He always had a complimentary slice waiting for him whenever he went to see the restaurant's owner.

And the rest of my family? Well, we just never really talk about it. I know that Mom goes to his grave in the morning and then eats a marble frosted donut by the lake in Bloomfield Park. Marble frosted were his favorite.

But this day hits me harder than it does my brothers. They all have families, people, and actives to keep them occupied. I've never had that before this year, and I can't seem to drag myself out of it despite having Ryan around. My bond with my father was complicated, but I was also the one who was there when he died. I saw it with my own eyes, and ...

I have to shut the thought down before it completely undoes me. Instead, I slap a pillow over my face and drift back off to sleep. The memories are too painful to relive.

"You could have told me today was the anniversary of his death," Ryan says quietly as I emerge from the dreamless sleep I was in.

Her keys are in her hand, and her face is a little red, so I know her workout must have ended just a little bit ago.

Sitting up, I wipe the exhaustion from my eyes and survey her wearily. "Never had anyone with me on this day before."

She kicks off her sneakers and crawls up the bed, planting herself next to me and then pulling me into her arms. It's not the hold of a lover, it's one of compassion ... which I didn't realize I needed until right now.

"You're grieving. It's nothing to hide. You don't have to talk about it, but I can be here for you."

God, I feel like a goddamn wimp. Tears threaten behind my eyeballs, and I burrow deeper into her chest, trying to take comfort in the warmth of her silky skin.

"Sometimes I wish my Dad were here, just so I could ask him if he was proud of my recovery. I'm not sure if he knew how bad my addiction was getting before he died. I was only twenty-two when he died, enrolled at the local public college, and I wasn't around for much of his last years. Part of me has always wanted to know what he would have done had he seen me spiral like I did. Or maybe, I wonder more, if I would have spiraled like that? My dad was a great father, but he could be harsh. He never hit us, but his words or lack of them could serve as an even swifter hand of punishment most times."

Ryan listens intently, letting me work out my own feelings on the subject.

"Would he have dragged me home by the ear and gone all Marine or some shit on me? Would he have locked me in a bathroom for three days to detox, and then told me to get my fucking life together? I think about it all the time; how, if he were still alive, maybe I wouldn't have gotten away with so much."

"I'm not sure that's a very fair judgment of what your mom and brothers did for you, though. They gave you space, stepped in when necessary, tried to allow you to mature and do things on your own. Some might argue that you had to hit rock bottom before you could improve your life."

She had a point. If my father had forced me to get clean, would it actually have lasted? I doubt it.

"I guess I just miss him. I'm the baby, the one who spent the most time clinging to his pant legs, following him around the office or listening to his deep philosophies on baseball strategies and using statistics to set a lineup. My older brothers were off and gone living their own lives before I could really remember, and Forrest was always in a world of his own. I probably spent the most time with my dad, alone, out of all of us. We fell into almost ... a friendship, when I wasn't out partying. All the time, I think about what he'd think of my woodworking, how he'd have helped me move into my first apartment."

Then Ryan says something that I think will stick with me for the rest of my life.

"I think trying to interpret what our parents would think of our life is the wrong way to go about it. Sure, I assume all parents have a vision of where they want their child's path to go.

But ... that isn't the point. Our choices and our dreams are. People waste a lot of time trying to please others, especially the ones responsible for creating them. If we spent half as much time just living for us ... we might all be a lot happier."

How did I find someone whose soul completely matches my own? I thought this on an almost daily basis, that's how much Ryan shocks me with the things she says. As if she and I share one brain.

And one heart.

30

"**A**ll right, bend it, bend it ... just a little more ..."

The piece fits snugly, exactly where I intended it to go, and I turn the welding torch off and flip my mask off.

"Damn, that looks nice." Stefan high fives me, his coveralls dirty as hell from the last two hours of grease and fire.

I huff out a breath, examining the work. "Yeah, it really does."

We've just finished bending one of the metal pieces into the circular face of the clock I'm due to deliver in a month and half's time. The piece was a coppery straight bar of steel that I used a saw and a torch to mold and sculpt into a line of flowers, shooting off in every direction from the center bar. It took me weeks to get the hang of the welding practices, but with some help from Stefan, the expert in that field, I pulled it off. The two semi-circles I created, from sketches of real flowers I found in Bloomfield Park, outline the face of the clock perfectly.

"Almost done now," my friend muses, plopping down on a stool and wiping the sweat from his brow.

He's not kidding. I can't believe how fast the last three

months have moved. What started as a conceptual idea then moved into the drawing and design stages, which led to picking out the materials. From there, I spent hours in my barn, cutting and sculpting, sanding and studying the inner workings of a clock. Forrest helped a ton because my brain just couldn't compute a lot of it, but the creativity was all me.

When it came time to start threading metal into my massive cube that would be installed on top of the tower on Main Street, I knew I needed help. So I called Stefan, a buddy I met at a local artist trade show near Philly.

And together, we've been working for the past few weeks to infuse copper into the stained wood design. It gives the clock an old-world feel, while also keeping it timeless. Not to be punny, or anything.

But it looks … damn good. I'm bragging, because yeah, I'm fucking proud. This project has been really tough to pull off, and by the time it gets hoisted up there with a crane and installed, it will be my biggest piece finished to date.

"Don't you have a hot date to get to?" Stefan looks at his phone and then holds it up for me to see.

"Oh, shit," I mutter, pulling the welding mask clear off my head as I start shrugging out of my dirty work jumpsuit.

"Yeah, don't make the mistake of standing your woman up. Especially in the early days. It'll leave you in the doghouse, bro." He chuckles to himself.

Stefan lives with his wife and two kids about an hour from here, and for as much as he talks crap about them, you can tell he's a dedicated family man.

"I don't plan to. I can make it to Ryan on time … if I do fifteen over the speed limit."

I slip into my boat shoes, comb my fingers through my hair, and leave Stefan to clean up. I know he'll take one for the team as he yells after me, "Don't kill anyone or get pulled over!"

Damn, I totally lost track of time. It's not that I forgot about our date, but I just got so wrapped up in what I was doing that the hours blended together. Ryan will forgive me if I'm a few minutes late; she loves how hard I'm working on the clock.

I make it to the sushi restaurant in twenty minutes, meaning I'm five minutes past the time my girlfriend and I decided on to meet for date night.

The minute I get out of my car, she's on me. It's only a joke, but this wouldn't be Ryan if she didn't rib me.

"I have to drive myself to the date and he's late. Jeez, not sure this guy is getting in my pants after this asshole behavior." She rolls those beautiful amber eyes, that tonight are lined with black kohl.

The makeup only enhances her minx-like beauty, intensifying every already knockout feature of her face. She's more dressed up than usual, probably because I'm finally taking her out of Fawn Hill. She's been asking for sushi for a month, and we don't have a local restaurant, so I finally ponied up and asked Forrest where he likes to go. So here we are, standing outside of an eatery I know I won't like, with Ryan in a leather mini-skirt that my dick can't seem to keep calm about.

"Where is he? Let me at him, I'll beat his ass." I hold up my dukes, and Ryan chuckles.

"Lost track of time?" She saunters to me on those fuck-me heels, wrapping her slender arms around my waist.

I nod, bending down to cover her mouth. God, she smells good … like warm chocolate chip cookies, the kind you can never just have one of. The kiss stretches on, until someone opens the door of the restaurant and almost hits Ryan in the back. The man walking out looks at us with a knowing smile, and I shuffle us backward as Ryan drops her forehead to my shirt.

"Well, guess that asshole might be getting to second base." I wiggle my eyebrows at her, and she hits my chest with a weak tap.

"Maybe even third, since he's taking me to eat sushi, which he claims he doesn't like." Ryan smiles over her shoulder as I hold the door open and we walk in.

I chuckle. "Can we stop talking about me in third person?"

"Yes, please. It's getting hard to keep up with." She laughs, agreeing, and we're led to our table. "So, I have the real story. I called Forrest, and he told me that you've never even tried sushi."

My jaw drops, but in good humor. "You called my twin? Behind my back? The nerve!"

Ryan gives me a sly smile. "He said that he brought Penelope here when they were dating because she claimed she didn't like it either. Now it's one of her favorite foods! So, I'm going to give you a crash course in raw fish."

Now it's my turn to school her. "I don't need any help when it comes to you and raw fish."

My tone is complete innuendo, and Ryan balls up the wrapper she just plucked off the end of the straw in her water and throws it at my head.

"You're a dirty man."

I run a finger up and down her wrist where it rests on the table. "And you like it."

"I'm not going to confirm or deny." She turns her attention to the menu in front of her.

I don't even bother, because I won't know what to order anyway. I'm here for her, because she's done so much for me. Staying in Fawn Hill, taking a job that is out of her norm, spending so much time with my family ... she's given up a lot to fit into my life. The least I can do is shove seaweed in my mouth for her.

Honestly, I'd do just about anything for her. My heart is a

beat up, scarred, mauled thing. Before her, it didn't beat correctly and barely felt. But with every touch, every whisper, every moment spent with her ... it has come alive. It's not perfectly healed, but it is hers. And ... she claims she wants it. Apparently, miracles do happen.

Ryan places our order and then squares her shoulders to grin at me. "I can't wait to watch you try this. You're going to fall in love."

I roll my eyes. "We'll see. Is it your favorite food?"

She tilts her head to the side, her eyes going to the ceiling in thought. "Hmm, no. The best meal I ever ate was at this little shack by the ocean in San Diego. This place was like, right off the highway. It literally shook every time a car drove by. But, they had the best scallop tacos I've ever eaten in my life. God, thinking about those just gives me a food orgasm."

Her joy about the food makes me smirk. She's so damn cute when she gets passionate about her travels. "If you could travel to one place in the world, where would it be?"

I ask because I know she loves this topic of conversation, and Ryan doesn't even hesitate.

"Well, I've already been there. *But*, I'd go back to The Maldives. It's the most beautiful place I've ever been in my life. The water is clear, the bluest blue you've ever had the honor to view."

"That rhymes." I lace our hands together on the table. "But it sounds picturesque."

Ryan regards me for a moment. "If you could travel to one place in the world, where would you go?"

She hasn't asked me this before. Normally, she'll just regale me with her tales of adventure, and I listen, truly interested. But now that she has, I'm stumped to realize I never thought about it.

It takes me a few moments, but then I speak. "I'm ... not sure.

Maybe Italy, or France. For the art. I'd love to see the ceiling in the Sistine Chapel, or some of the works in the Louvre. I'd like to see these pieces that are so iconic, that were made centuries ago."

Ryan nods, grinning from ear to ear. "The artist seeking his passion."

"Something like that." I nod. "But, that'll take a lot of clock towers. You know anyone else looking for a new one?"

Ryan taps her chin. "Not that I can think of. But, don't worry … someday, we'll go see those places. Together."

It's the first time she's said the word someday, and my heart begins to bloom with the possibility.

31

Fletcher and I lay in bed after having sex, our labored breathing mingling as our legs tangle in each other and the sheets.

He brushes my hair behind my ear, a quiet smile ghosting over his lips.

"What's going on in that head of yours?" I ask, curious.

While he's always honest, there are a lot of moments where Fletcher goes quiet. I've learned this about him in the time we've spent together. I've never asked why, but I think he's trying to fight away those demons in his mind. Should I tell him I know all too well what that's like?

"Why did it take us so long, do you think?" he asks, twirling a lock of hair in his finger.

"Why do you think it got so deep, so quickly?" Because to me, everything seemed to happen so fast.

Fletcher seems to ignore my question. "I think ... I've spent a lot of the last few years denying myself every urge. The urge to drink, the urge to fuck, the urge to get close to someone or make something of myself. See, Ryan, my brain has taught itself that when I really do want something, it's probably bad for me. Alcohol? Ruined my fucking life and I wanted every drop of it desperately. From there, every base need was detrimental, and it stripped away who I was, right to the core. I had to build myself back up. I wanted to be worthy of you, Ryan."

I love that he only calls me by my name, and not babe or baby or sweetheart. I've wanted to hear those endearments from men in my past, but the fact that he says my full name every time he's talking to me ... it almost seems more intimate.

And the confession ... *my lord.*

A streak of moonlight dusts over his hair as I skim his temple with my thumb. "You're more than worthy. The way your brain works, my brain works."

"Is it too fast for you?" He pulls me in closer, if that's even possible with how snug our bodies are fit against each other right now.

I don't need to think before I shake my head. "Maybe a part of me was delaying the inevitable. I think we both know that there is ... something unspoken that connects us. I thought I knew what having a spark with someone was like, but this is different. When I saw you for the first time, there was just this ... shift. Not one that was difficult, or some flame that I was trying to keep alive ... it was just *there.* This constant buzz that I knew would be so *right* when I finally acknowledged it, but that's the thing, isn't it? Sometimes we avoid the things we know will complete us because we think we're not ready."

Fletcher's eyes bore into mine. "I'm ready."

In the quiet of our bedroom, I feel more vulnerable than I have in my entire life. Like a nerve that's been exposed, trying not to get shocked.

"Me too," I whisper.

Looking at him, I know I am. Maybe I had to go through those bad times, the periods of my life when I thought I'd never find someone to truly love me ... that I'd never find someone to be my family.

But what I'd said to Fletcher at the restaurant had been true; I had been looking for someday, and with him, I could finally picture it.

After a long day of teaching, which is really only eight to one but feels like three years, I head to Presley's studio for a much-needed yoga practice.

My muscles are tense and stiff after a day trying to get through to stubborn pre-teens, and nothing relaxes me more than down dogs and child's poses. That isn't to say I don't really enjoy what I'm doing. When Hattie used her pull to get me hired on as an aide to Mr. Billings, the middle school computer teacher, I was a little hesitant. A job here, especially one in the school district, meant permanence. But for the last two months, it has been going rather well. I enjoy getting up the three days a week that I help Billings and interacting with the kids. I'm more of an adult friend to them than a teacher, and it's why they're all clambering to tell me their ridiculous pre-teen drama.

Secretly, I love it. This is the best job I've had in years, and it's opening my eyes to just what life could be like if I stay in Fawn Hill.

Not that I have any intention of going anywhere, anytime soon. Fletcher and I spend every night together, and I'm so close to telling him I love him, it freaks me the hell out. In a good way.

Because I know now that I've never truly been in love. Not in this *complete* way, where it's as if the man is the other half of my soul, walking around just waiting to be connected to me. When I'm not with Fletcher, it's like a part of me is dimmed. I'm both shaken by and addicted to the feeling of needing him as entirely as I do.

Pushing through the front doors of Presley's studio, a calmness sweeps over me. That's what she's designed the aesthetic to do, put her clients at peace, but I'm always amazed at how much stress comes off my shoulders the minute I walk through the entrance.

Abigail, Presley's lone employee, sits behind the desk that's flanked with racks of soft tank tops and stretchy pants for purchase.

"Hey, Abby. Presley in the back?" I ask, setting my shoes and bag in a cubby.

She shakes her head, the dark dreads she sports shaking like one of those dogs that looks like yarn. "Nah, she called out. Has me covering her classes. Think she might be sick or something."

A frown has my lips turning down, because that's unlike Presley. First of all, she's that freak of a friend that we all have who never gets sick. The entire island of Manhattan could have the flu, and she's healthy as a spring daisy.

The nagging feeling stays with me throughout the workout, making it impossible to calm down and give in to the peaceful burn of the exercise. I take off early, forgoing the breathing exercise that Abigail takes the class through as they lie on their yoga mats with their eyes closed.

It takes me ten minutes to walk to Presley and Keaton's house, and I realize that soon, the weather will turn much colder. We're into October now, and I'll have to figure out a car situation. Walking through Fawn Hill in the snow and slush is not my idea of fun.

Using the key I still have, I let myself in through their front door, and call her name.

"Pres?" I don't yell it in case she's sleeping.

A sound catches my attention, and it sounds like a hiccup. Calling her name again, I listen closer, and I hear someone crying.

Following the sobbing sound, I find Presley kneeling on the tile floor of her bathroom, tears leaking down her face.

"Pres! What's wrong? Are you hurt?" My voice is frantic in my ears as I sink to my knees beside her.

She hiccups on a sob and offers up her hand. There is an object in it, and I tear my eyes from her face to look at it.

"It's negative," she cries, handing me the pregnancy test.

I take it, careful not to touch the end she inevitably peed on. Sure enough, there is only one line, not two like the simple test instructs there should be if a woman is carrying a baby.

"Oh, Pres ..." I whisper, momentarily stunned.

I wasn't even aware they were trying, and with the utter devastation marking her features, I can tell this is not the first negative test she's gotten back.

"I wasn't even sure I wanted kids, you know? Before I met Keaton, I wasn't sure that having a family was in the cards for me. But then he kept talking about how beautiful our little girl would be someday, or how much he wanted to play baseball with his son. And I could see that, I could picture it *so* clearly. And then my arms started feeling ... lonely. As if I was just waiting for something to fill them. For a baby to be rocked in them. I've never felt such a sharp stab of longing before in my life. So, we started trying. I was so excited at first, so hopeful. It was flirty and fun, and Keaton was so thrilled he could burst at the seams. But ... it's been eight months. And I just keep getting my period or peeing on these fucking sticks and being told by a piece of plastic that my womb is hopelessly empty."

She breaks down into heart-wrenching sobs, and I herd her into my arms. I hold my friend as the sadness wracks her body, and I grieve for her. I can't imagine what it's like to not be able to get pregnant, when all of your hope is riding on this tiny window of a miracle.

It's at this moment that I realize ... the happy ending doesn't mean a person's world lives on enchantedly ever after. The wrapped-up-in-a-bow ending isn't a cure-all for misfortune and struggle.

Here I was, idolizing and envying Presley because she got the man and all she ever wanted. I thought that the Nash brothers and their wives were all just blissfully, annoyingly happy at all times. But, that wasn't the truth. Everyone had problems, even the ones who found their soul mates and perfect careers.

It makes me both resolved and upset. I've been trying so hard to fix everything I thought was wrong with myself, contend with the demons inside me to expel them from my mind and heart. So that I could feel nothing but sheer certainty when it came to being with Fletcher. So that I didn't regret breaking my promise or leaving the life I'd worked so hard for behind.

Finding Presley like this? It makes me realize that I don't have to be perfect to be loved. But it also makes me terrified that when I finally do give myself to the person I'm truly meant to be with, it won't be enough.

How can life throw terrible things your way when you finally find the happy ending?

That niggle of doubt that creeps into my heart is dangerous. It festers, infecting the love that's sprouted there even before I know it's wreaking havoc.

S *crape.*

"Fuck." A giggle.

Bang.

"Oh, shit ..." Another giggle.

I rise from my position on the couch, where I'd been lounging, watching baseball, and walk to the front door of the apartment. When I unlock it and pull it open, a drunk Ryan is standing on the other side.

"Hey, babe." She hiccups, which makes her giggle again.

Her lipstick is smudged, and she's removed her heels on the short walk home from the Goat, and she looks so adorably silly right now that I want to carry her to the bedroom.

Problem is, she smells like a bottle of tequila, and immediately my hackles rise.

"Hi, beautiful. Have fun tonight?" I try to keep my voice light with amusement.

She stumbles into the apartment, throwing her bag and shoes on the ground and then unbuttoning her jeans, because why not.

"Oh, gosh, *yes*. I love girl's night. Don't you love girl's night?

Just a bunch of bitches gathering around to gossip. And drink. And talk about men. And drink."

"Yeah, you mentioned that." I can't help but chuckle as she moseys through our home, throwing her clothes haphazardly as she undresses.

"Come, sit down, while I regale you." Ryan tries to throw a sexy look my way, but almost trips over her own two feet.

I should keep my distance, but she's allowed to get drunk with her friends. It's not her problem that I can't control the urge inside me. So I sit on the bed, watching as she takes out her big hoop earrings.

Before I know what's happening, though, Ryan is crawling up the bed toward me.

She straddles my lap, and instantly, my cock is straining to be inside her. How the hell does she do this to me? I've had plenty of experience, not much that I remember but I do, but no one compares to the speed in which Ryan can get me hot and bothered.

It could also be the fact that I was celibate for five damn years, but we don't need to mention that now.

I can smell the booze on her breath, and I know that if she kisses me, I'll be able to taste the bitter fire of a margarita on her lips. Part of me wants to, so desperately wants to get just a lick of my old friend. My mistress, alcohol, the woman who led me to such highs and such lows.

Fumbling in my pocket, I grab at the chip. Five years sober. Not a drop of that poison in one thousand, eight hundred and twenty-five days. Or a little bit more than that. It takes every ounce of strength and willpower in me to push a horny, sexy-as-hell Ryan from my lap.

Her frown is exaggerated in her drunken state. "What's wrong, baby?"

"Not tonight, babe. Why don't we just go to sleep?" I smile at her, trying to shrug her off as she begins pulling at my pajama bottoms.

"You don't want me?" Her smile is naughty, and while she probably thinks she's being coy, she's too inebriated to be subtle.

Gently, I push her hands away. "Ry ... not tonight. You're drunk."

"And? It means you can take advantage of me." She starts to take her top off, and I groan as her perky little nipples poke out from the see-through lace bra she's wearing. "I was thinking about you all night. About how I wanted to come home and get on top of you. How I wanted your tongue in my pussy."

Jesus Christ, this woman is going to kill me. Because if there is anything that has a stronger pull over me than alcohol, it's Ryan.

But I can smell the scent of her drinks everywhere, and I know that if I don't get out of this room, something bad will happen.

"I can't ... kiss you right now. You've been drinking. I can't even smell it. It's hard for me to even stand here with you. I'm sorry, babe ... I just can't."

Her cheekbones, which were slanted upward in a sly grin, immediately lower. Her eyes lose a little bit of their playful light, and this is exactly what I didn't want to happen. Because of my shit, my past, I'm ruining her good time.

"I'm so sorry, Fletch, I forgot. I didn't even think, of course, you don't want to taste that. Shit, I'll go brush my teeth ..."

She flees into the bathroom, but I move quickly to her, catch her arm. "It's okay. I'm just going to sleep on the couch. You take the bed."

"You're not going to even sleep with me?" Her voice takes on a note of hurt, and it guts me that I put it there.

This was bound to happen, I knew it from the start. My issues would make her feel unwanted or put pain in her eyes.

Because I was weak, I would have to shut myself off from her. Because I wasn't strong enough of a person, of a man, I'd have to put my own needs ahead of hers.

"I can't, the smell ..." I try to explain with a wave of my arm through the air.

Ryan retreats even further into herself, those amber eyes going midnight black, her arms crossing over her naked torso. "Got it. I can just leave."

"No, please stay. I want to know that you're safe. And this is your home too. I want you in our bed." I still linger by the door instead of hugging her in my arms, because I don't trust myself.

"Just not enough to want to get in it with me," she spits, and I know she wouldn't say it if she wasn't drunk.

But it's half-true what they say; alcohol loosens your tongue to say the things you wouldn't if you were sober. And Ryan's accusation only proves to me that she doesn't fully understand how fragile and important my sobriety is.

"I'll be out there if you need anything." I hang my head, turning to go.

She harrumphs, and I can sense that all too irrational anger that liquor brings out in a person. "And I guess I'll jump in the shower since you can't stand me right now."

The alcohol is blurring her rationale, but it still doesn't keep the sting of betrayal from entering my veins. I thought that Ryan understood my battle to keep my life clean, but with a few harsh lashes of her tongue, she's undone some level of trust there had been between us.

I sleep on the couch, the cold leather seeping into my bones, listening to Ryan breath softly in our bed.

Alone.

I wake up in a dismal fog of tequila scent and nausea.

The two make a disastrous combination, and I'm running for the bathroom the minute my eyes blink open toward the ceiling. Falling to my knees on the cold tile floor, I heave the contents of my stomach into the toilet bowl before wiping my mouth and reaching a hand up to flush.

"You okay?" Fletcher says from the doorway of the bathroom, and I nod weakly.

Fuck, what did I drink last night? "Sorry you had to see that."

"Don't apologize for not feeling well." His tone holds a gentle soothing, but there is an edge to it.

"I can when I did it to myself," I argue, standing on wobbly legs.

"Come sit, I'll make you some toast. Best hangover cure I know. That and tomato juice."

Just the thought of the acidic drink makes my stomach roll. "Please don't mention V8 again."

He nods, and I slip into the bedroom to pull one of his over-sized T-shirts over my naked body. I feel like someone slammed a two-by-four into the side of my head, and by the way Fletcher is acting, I know I said some stupid shit last night.

Passing the couch, I see the blankets folded on top of a pillow. A memory comes back to me, in hazy hues, but it's there. Fletcher telling me I was drunk, him pushing me away, and then going to sleep on the couch.

Fuck, I really messed up. I'm pretty sure I yelled at him, when I should have been understanding. *Of course,* he wouldn't want to taste alcohol on my tongue. It would be a trigger for him to sleep next to me all night, smelling the tequila wafting off of me.

And here I'd gone, cutting him down because of it.

No, not because of him. Because the minute he told me that I was drunk, that he couldn't be around me ...

He reminded me of a life he'd never been a part of. One where my mother would push me away, because she loved the high more than she loved me. In my warped brain, in my drunken state of mind ... that's what I'd thought Fletcher was doing. His addiction was causing him to push me away, and I snapped at him as if he was my deadbeat biological parent.

I lower myself into a chair, rubbing my arms that are now peppered with goose bumps. He's in there making me toast right now, and I don't deserve the kindness.

"The reason I got so angry ..." I trail off, not sure I'm ready to have this conversation.

Everything has been going so well. We've been shacked up for months, I'm a solid part of his life, and he is in mine. I've established myself here, and we're ... happy. Every so often, I have to ignore the whispers from the back of my mind that tell me I'm doing exactly what I did with Yanis. But other than that, life is amazing.

But life can't be amazing without putting all your cards on the table. And I've left my biggest ace off of it. Fletcher still doesn't know about my past, and it's about time I told him about it.

Fletcher walks out of the tiny galley kitchen, holding the plate with my toast, his eyes a stormy, clouded blue today.

"Do you want to talk about it?" he asks gently.

My eyes study his, looking from one blue orb to the next. I'm not sure where to start, so I pick a point and run with it.

"I went to Greece on a project that my boss put me up for. Honestly, I didn't even want to go. That sounds so selfish now, who doesn't want to go to Greece? But I'd just gotten back from a long-term project in Norway and was looking forward to the summer in New York. But, I'd flown out reluctantly, and my boss had promised to pay for a fabulous Airbnb to start my trip off right. I met Yanis three days in and fell completely head over heels. He was a local artist whose paintings had begun to gain traction all over Europe. He was charismatic, devilishly sexy, and complimented me so much, that at times I thought he was forcing it a bit. But ... he looked like a soldier from the movie *300*, and I was alone in a new place. One date blended into three, and by the second month of my project, we were living together. Looking back, I barely knew the guy. It was all so exotic and romantic, which tends to be my downfall. And life was just one big romantic comedy. Come on ... living in Greece, on the arm of an artist, it was whimsical. We were together for a year and a half before I found him in our bed, having a threesome with two local models. The truth is ... I knew it was happening. Somewhere deep inside your soul, you always do. It's hard not to know if your partner is distant, or not as touchy-feely. We all ignore it, chalk it up to long-term companionship ... but I knew. I just didn't want to see it."

Fletcher doesn't reach for my hand, but instead, keeps his steady gaze pinned on me. He doesn't interrupt either ... and maybe he knows I need to spit this out more than I realize.

"That's what I do. I fall into relationships so quickly because I want ... hell, I'm not sure sometimes. Love? Someone to be singularly focused on me. A person to call my own? Remember I told you I grew up in foster care?"

The brief register of sympathy on his face tells me that he feels sad for me, but he schools his features and nods his head, urging me to go on.

"My mother abandoned me at a supermarket when I was five. Just walked me in, took me to the cereal aisle, and went to go score. She was, and still is, a junkie. I stared at the Lucky Charms box so long, I thought my eyes were becoming kaleidoscopes. It wasn't until the store was closing for the night that one of the employees found me, called the cops to come and get me. I floated in and out of the system from then on. Going into foster homes, some okay and some worse. Nothing absolutely horrible ever happened to me. No, the scars that remain are from something much worse ... complete isolation. Most times, I was just ignored. No one spoke to me or listened. I made no friends because I moved around from home to home so much, and there was not one person in my life who was a constant fixture."

His fingers thread through mine. "I ... didn't know it was that bad."

Shaking my head, I look away, another wave of nausea hitting me. "No one really does. Presley knows, but she's probably one of the only ones. I ... don't like to talk about it. Don't like to dwell on it because I should be so grateful for the life I've created for myself. How can this woman, who doesn't give a shit about me, still take up such a big portion of my headspace? It's crazy."

Unshed tears form a lump in my throat. "I'm so ashamed of how I acted last night. I lashed out at you because you pushed me away, just like she did, while dealing with your own demons. Demons that *she* has. It's all a twisted mess, and rationally, it shouldn't matter. But emotions never listen to silly little things like that, do they? I'm so sorry, Fletcher. I'm fucked up."

I breakdown into sobs, because I feel like last night veered us so off course. I'm not a crier, I rarely ever do ... but this has been coming. Something had to come to a head, and even if the events of last night seem like a molehill, they were part of the larger mountain. Fletcher's reaction set off a tsunami.

"Shh, it's okay. I've got you. I've got you."

He holds me until the tears dry up, but after they're gone, I can feel the tide has shifted.

There is a void.

Ever since the morning Ryan told me about her mother, about why she freaked out when I slept on the couch, there has been this distance between us that neither of us can seem to bridge.

We're not talking about it, either, which only makes it worse. I'm not sure if she's more upset about her own reaction, or if she's slowly realizing what a life with me would actually look like.

I don't have free rein to indulge my every whim, which in turn means neither does my partner. My personality, the addict switch in my brain, can't handle it. I can't even smell alcohol in my apartment, and I'm not sure Ryan ever thought about that before the other night.

The only way I can think to explain it to her, and maybe end this awkward tension between us, is to take her to a meeting.

"I don't need to come, really. If this is your space ..."

It's the second time Ryan has said as much, as we walk the short distance down the sidewalk on Main Street to the church where my AA meetings are held. And because it's not the first time she's mentioned it, I feel myself grind down on my back molars.

"Do you not want to go? Because I thought this might be good for us, after the other night."

Something has stilted between us, as if all the air has gone out of our relationship, leaving it hard to breathe. We're not functioning normally, and though her confession about her biological mother opened up another side of her to me, it also left a hollowness. Because now I know, I remind her of the parent who abandoned her.

Her amber eyes flit to mine, and she's chewing on her lip so hard, I'm surprised it's not bleeding. "No, I do. It's just ... I won't know how to act."

That really pisses me off. "Why, because recovering alcoholics are a bunch of savages? What does that even mean? You're there to support me, to observe how I heal myself. You sit next to me and listen. No one is asking you to swing from vines or slit open a vein."

She takes two steps away from me, and when I look down into her face, it's as if I've slapped her. Immediately, I want to comfort her, but I'm hurting, too.

"That's ... I didn't mean that. Of course, I'm here to support you." But by the way her voice shakes, it doesn't seem that she's totally convinced herself of that, either.

They say the honeymoon period ends sometime, and I think ours is about up.

We're silent as we walk into the church, and I head for the basement stairs and down to the auxiliary room where our meetings are held. On the way in, I say hi to a couple of people, not introducing Ryan because this is supposed to be anonymous. Not that she won't recognize them from town, but what goes on inside these walls is supposed to be kept inside these walls.

The room is dank, and the smell gives every indication of just how old the building is. Rot and burnt coffee fill your nostrils, and the sound of metal folding chairs scraping across the linoleum floors is the music I associate with AA meetings.

Ryan sticks close to my side, even though I don't lace my hand in hers like I normally would. We just feel off, and it's making me distant. There is one person I need to introduce her to, though.

Cookie walks in, a cloud of cigarette smoke seeming to still surround her, and she's in her usual getup. Clunky boots, dark black jeans, a sweater that rides too low on her chest, and some kind of vibrant costume necklace slung around her neck. She's fabulous with a take-no-prisoners attitude, and I can see a bit of how Ryan will act when she's close to her age.

"Cook," I call, motioning her over. When she reaches us, a brow raised, I introduce them. "This is Ryan, my girlfriend. And Ryan, this is Cookie, my sponsor."

Cookie's face is expressionless as Ryan extends her hand. "Hey, it's really nice to finally meet you. Fletcher talks about you all the time."

"Hmm, hopefully nice things." My sponsor tries for unimpressed.

Ryan is a confident woman, not one to take crap, but she's so out of her element right now that I think Cookie rattles her.

"Oh, of course. He says you saved his life," Ryan gushes, and it's so unlike her.

I want to joke that she's being a kiss ass, because she's not even this flattering to my mother, but it's probably not a good time to point that out.

"I'd expect that you wouldn't screw it up, then." Cookie eyes her with a presumptive glance, and I feel the need to get in the middle before these two start fighting like turkey vultures over a deer carcass.

That deer carcass being me, because hell if I'm even worth this much passive aggression.

"Let's ... find our seats." I steer Ryan away from Cookie, looking back to give my sponsor a glare that says "behave."

"Well, she's a peach." Ryan snorts.

"She's just being protective." Although, I have no idea why. She's the one who told me to start dating.

"I know that." My girl's voice rings of hurt.

The meeting begins, and a bunch of people stand up to share. I decided before we got here that I'd hang back, because I've already shared a lot of my worst behavior with Ryan, and we're already on rocky ground. I don't need to add to the tension by spilling my past indiscretions; it's big enough that she even came here with me.

Except, when I look over at her halfway through the meeting, I can read the judgment all over her face. Oh, sure, she is trying to mask it, but I can read her so well after the time we've spent together. Ryan is uncomfortable, unconsciously twisting in her seat and trying to avoid eye contact with everyone. It is clear what she's thinking; every one of these people reminds her of her mother. These are addicts, thieves, cheaters, gamblers of security and love.

Which means ... that's how she looks at me. I see her jaw tic and her fingers tap rhythmically on her leg as each person tells of their failures or successes since the last meeting.

Turning away from her, I try to immerse myself in the meeting. If she isn't going to support me in this, I don't see how we can get over the rut we're stuck in. But I do know that I need meetings to help me stay sober, so I pay attention and block Ryan and her meltdown out.

When the session comes to a close, I stand up, talking a little with the other members around me and then saying the serenity prayer before it really ends. Ryan looks about ready to bolt, but I want to talk to Cookie first.

"Perhaps it's time that I talked to your belle." Cookie raises an eyebrow when I reach her at the folding table, stirring her coffee.

The coffee here is shit, which is notorious at AA meetings, but it's better than nothing. "Lay off her, Cook."

My sponsor shrugs. "She looked like she saw a damn ghost that whole meeting. Her parents abuse her? Or were they drunks?"

I try not to let my surprise register. "How could you tell that?"

"Because my kid looked at me that way for the longest time. You don't want her looking at you like that. Or worse, thinking she has a handle on it until you're in too deep, and she breaks your damn heart, Fletch."

Too bad she already held that power. "I ... things aren't as rosy as they once were."

My sponsor smiles a small smile, like my sentiment is all too familiar to her. "They never are. That's love, though. You're not supposed to feel its wrath in the good times. It's the rough waters that are hardest to navigate, and you're going through your first storm right here. I'm not sure what happened, Fletcher, but there are some fundamental issues between you two. You're an addict, and she's terrified of addicts. It's something you'll have to address."

She's right, of course. Though I wish we could just go back, stay in that honeymoon period a little longer.

My whole life has been choppy waters ... it was nice to have blue skies for the little time I had them.

36

I t's been three days since I went to Fletcher's AA meeting, and we still haven't talked about it.

Things are tense and strained, and we're barely even speaking to each other. I'm still staying nights at his place because that's what I do. I hold on until the end, until my heart is teetering on the edge of broken.

This time is different, though. With every second that passes where we don't address the elephant in the room, my shoulders slump a little more with the weight of failure. Fletcher and I have some serious, foundational issues to talk over. He's trying to keep his sobriety, and I've dealt my whole life with caring for someone who was in and out of drug highs. Fletcher wants space when he's struggling, and I need reassurance when it comes to my abandonment and relationship problems of the past.

We're two sides of a coin, trying to become one, and neither of us wants to rock the boat for fear of sinking us both.

I'm sitting on the couch, waiting for Fletcher to get home from another late barn shift working on the clock, when my phone rings.

It's Geralyn, and I curse, knowing that she called me twice this week and I haven't called her back. My old boss, or current boss ... I'm not even really sure what's going on. I'm still on her roster of employees, though she's been great in giving me my space. But with my new position at the school, I'm not sure I can even be one of her coders anymore, and I've been too chicken to have that conversation.

Clicking the little green phone icon bouncing on my screen, I pick up. "Hey, Geralyn!"

"Ryan, where the hell have you been?" she starts right in, her tone a new level of pissed off.

I cringe. "I've been busy here—"

I'm about to explain myself, but she cuts me off. "In bumble-fuck Georgia?"

My eyebrows knot in confusion. "I'm in Pennsylvania ..."

"Whatever, who cares. What does matter is that I have a job for you. Big system setup in Denmark, private security firm that needs an impenetrable system. I told them you'd be there in two days."

"Sorry, Ger, I'm still out of the game." I shrug as if she can see me on the other end of the phone.

Her voice rings through in harsh, cutting tones. "Cut the crap, Ry. I want you on the next plane to Copenhagen. I need my best person on this, and that's you. Now, I've given you as much time as I can spare, but I need you to do this job."

My heart stutters, and it takes me a moment to suck in a breath. "Ger, I ... I really appreciate how much you've worked with my schedule the past couple of months. But I can't just pick up and go to Denmark."

"Why not? That's what you do, Ryan!" She sounds exasperated.

No, that's what I did. That's what I want to tell her. And even though I've contemplated in my head where I've ended up in the past few months, and tried to convince myself Fawn Hill was not that place ... I find that when faced with a choice, I don't want to leave.

Copenhagen is beautiful, I've been there twice. And at any other time of my life, I wouldn't hesitate. But somehow, this place, this small town in Pennsylvania, has gotten a hold on my heart. The sense of community among the people here, my group of Nash ladies and their men ...

Fletcher.

That's the number one reason, right there. I can't leave ... because I'm in love.

We might be having a rough time of it, but I've never wanted anything more than I want Fletcher. I know that now. Yanis and my past boyfriends could break my heart in a million different ways combined, and none of it would come close to equaling the devastating fallout that leaving Fletcher would cause.

If I tell her that, she'll scoff in my face. Because she's heard it before; Geralyn has known me long enough to know that I fall in and out of love as quickly as the seasons change.

But this time is different. When faced with my job and traveling the world, or staying here and being with Fletcher ...

I'd pick him. I can honestly say that's never been my choice before.

"I'm sorry, Ger, I can't go. I can try to do the work remotely—"

She cuts me off. "Ryan, they want you there in person. I've already sold them on the idea of a badass female coder. So pack your bags, pull up your big girl panties, and get flying. If you don't, I'll have to fire you and sue for breach of contract. Love ya!"

The dial tone hits me in the ear with a rude wail, and I pull the receiver away, my mouth still hanging open.

And as if timing wasn't already kicking me in the ass, Fletcher decides to walk in the door right at this moment.

He catches sight of my expression, probably one of horrified shock, and quickly sets his things down and shrugs out of his coat.

"What's wrong? Was it ... was it your mom?" It's the first time he's brought her up since I told him about my childhood.

"No ..." I rub my jaw, trying to wake myself from the daze Geralyn left in her demanding wake. "That was Geralyn, my boss. She wants me on a job."

"Oh." Fletcher sits down on the couch next to me, leaning back in surprise. "That's not what I thought you were going to say."

"Yeah .. I, uh, kind of blanked my job out the past couple of months. But she's insisting. Says she'll sue me if I don't show up."

"Well, then, you have to go, right?" Fletcher's voice gets scratchy. "Where is the job?"

"Denmark." My eyes flick to his, and I think we're both mirroring the same look of worry.

His gaze averts first, shifting to the side. "Damn ... that's not ... close. I thought you'd say New York or something."

I feel it, the slip. It begins, a sludging, nauseating slide from my throat, past my heart, into the pit of my stomach. It's our relationship, just falling out of my grasp. I could almost see it, the tips of my hands trying to catch it before it fell and smashed all over the floor.

"Come to Denmark with me." I grab Fletcher's hands, the idea taking flight in my chest.

We could travel together, he could see the art he's always wanted to see. I could get the job done, and then we'll come back. Together. As long as we were together, it didn't matter. I could support the two of us with whatever I was making on this project.

And maybe this could help us get through the bad period we are in. Getting out of Fawn Hill, a change of scenery, it could do wonders for us.

"Ryan, I can't leave Fawn Hill. I have the clock tower going up in a month's time. My family is here. I have an apartment I work hard to afford, and ... I love it here. This is where I belong."

I swear, my heart shatters into a million tiny shards. The glass of the splintered organ breaks haphazardly, and I know it will never fully be pieced together after this.

"Is this because your boss is making you go, or do you want to leave after what you saw in my meeting?" His eyes narrow.

Immediately, anger bubbles up in the back of my throat. First, he's saying he won't come with me, and now, he's accusing me of running away because AA spooked me into the next galaxy.

But this is my out, whether I'm being forced into it or not, and we both know it. I saw him in that meeting days ago, and I freaked the fuck out. But he also doesn't want to come with me. And that causes me to go into self-preservation mode.

"You know what? I think this was all a really terrible idea. You're right. I always jump into things, and this was no different. We felt the lust, we fucked, and then I got in deep because ... well, like I said, it's what I do. I should go, we're on the verge of breaking up anyway."

Fletcher looks as if I've sunk a knife right through his heart. "We are? Good to know your view on things. You never intended to stay here, did you? You can't even look at me after that meeting, after learning what I *really* am. Just because one addict abandoned you, doesn't mean another wouldn't try to love you the hardest he could for the rest of your life. You're right, you should go. Run away from your problems, like you always do. I don't need this bullshit."

"Fletcher ..." My voice is pure panic, and tears leak from the corners of my eyes. The thoughts racing in my head are telling me to deflect, defend ... but then they're telling me to try with all my might to save this. To save us.

"Go, Ryan. Just go."

I want to take it back, to tell him I didn't mean any of what I'd just said. But it was out there now, as were his words. I'm not sure how this did a one-eighty in three seconds flat, but then again, I have a penchant for burning my life to the ground quickly.

And now I'd be on to a new city, a fresh start. That was the way things always went.

Except this time, I know I won't be mending a broken heart.

I'd simply be limping along, trying to ignore the earthquake-sized tremors of an organ that would never repair itself.

37

FLETCHER

T wo weeks.

      Fourteen days.

      Three hundred and thirty-six hours.

That's how long Ryan has been gone, and how long I've been numb to everything around me.

I stare up at the ceiling of Keaton's guest room, because my brothers made me move in here after she left in fear I'd do something stupid. Truthfully, I'm glad they basically forced me into observational confinement. In those first few hours after she stormed out of my apartment, I was so close to hightailing it to the liquor store and guzzling a bottle of whiskey right there in the aisle.

But Keaton had come knocking, packed me a bag, and physically removed me from my apartment. I'd find out later that Ryan went running to Presley, who drove her to the airport and saw her off on the plane to New York, where she'd connect to Copenhagen.

The world seems dimmer without her here, and most days, I find it difficult to put two feet on the floor and keep moving. This is why they tell recovering alcoholics not to fall in love in the first year. Maybe the disclaimer should be not to fall in love ever, because it's too triggering to fall out of it.

Not that I have fallen out of it. My heart still burns with the memory of her, and I haven't fully convinced it that she's never coming back. Part of me hopes that she'll walk through the door and hand me my ass, tell me I fucked up and owe her an apology.

But she's a world away, and it's an important day for me. One I've been looking forward to. So, why do I feel nothing but pain as I dress for the ceremony in the dark gray button down and dark jeans our resident fashion advisor, Penelope, gave me as a present a week ago.

"Big day, Fletch." Presley grins a little as I walk into their kitchen.

She and I haven't seen much of each other since Ryan left, mostly because I'm avoiding her in her own home. I know she wants to be there for her best friend and her brother-in-law, and I don't want to make it harder for her. I'm the guy who broke her friend's heart, told her to leave. But Ryan wasn't innocent in this, and I think my brother's wife knows that.

"Yep." I try to smile, but it comes off as more of a grimace.

I pour myself a mug of coffee, chug it, and then stomach a piece of toast. Not only am I nursing one hell of a battered heart, but I'm also nervous as fuck.

Today is the day of the clock tower unveiling, and I'm terrified the damn thing won't work. Or it will look awful, or that the people in town will hate it. I've been jumpy since I tried to lie down and sleep last night, and it only intensifies when I get in the back seat of Keaton's truck and ride with him and Presley to the ceremony.

My mom is standing front and center when we get to Main Street, and a few of my friends wave or cheer quietly, anticipating the reveal.

"Hi, Ma." I kiss her on the cheek.

"Oh, I'm so proud of you. This is wonderful," she squeals.

"It's covered by a black curtain. You haven't even seen it yet ..." I mutter, trying not to get my hopes up.

There is a chance that everyone will think it's terrible.

"But I know the kind of work you do, and I already know it's beautiful," she says with a know-it-all nod that only a mother can give.

I shrug as Forrest, Penelope, and the kids walk up.

"You ready, bro?" My twin shakes my shoulders, jostling me.

"Uncle Fletch, you built this?" Matthew says in awe, though the clock is still covered.

I had him out to the barn in the final stages, because the little man seems interested in working with his hands. He helped me screw on the big hand of the clock, an ornate wood piece that I carved the founding date of Fawn Hill into.

"Sure did. Next one, you'll build." I wink at him.

"All right, everyone, can I have your attention?" Keaton says into a microphone, and the whole thing feels very grand.

My brother decided to appoint himself emcee of the unveiling, just like he basically appointed himself mayor of the town. I didn't mind though, it felt nice to have my sibling proud of me for a change.

"I am so glad we're all here to view the new clock tower today, but it's an even bigger day for our family. Fletcher has been honing his craft for a few years, and when he was awarded the project, I knew he'd do the best job. He has built us a gorgeous clock, one that will make Fawn Hill proud every time it chimes on the hour. Fletcher, we love you, and we're so proud of you."

My family whoops and hollers, shaking me as I throw up a sheepish wave to the crowd that's clapping around us.

Then everyone is counting down, and Bowen pulls the cord to the drape ...

The moment the curtain drops, and the minute hand starts ticking, I don't see the clock face.

In my mind, I only see her face.

"Wow, it looks amazing." Penelope smiles at me.

Forrest claps me on the shoulder. "Epic job, bro."

Mom has tears in her eyes when she hugs me. "I will cherish every time I look at it on my morning walk. I'll always see you on Main Street, now."

"I wish Ryan were here to see this," Presley mutters sadly, and Penelope leads her away by the elbow.

My heart drops to my feet when my sister-in-law says that, because I wish she was, too.

"You're a fucking moron." Forrest rounds on me, shaking his head.

"What?" I throw my arms up. "Do we have to do this today? You do all realize I just accomplished something huge."

"You told her to go. You got mad, acted like a child, and told her to go to Denmark." Bowen fills in the blank, and they all stare at me like I should be grounded.

"Do you think that being in love is easy? It's fucking hard. Especially with Penelope. Never fall in love with her, woman is barking mad," Forrest quips, and Keaton shoots him a glare.

My twin continues. "But seriously, being in a relationship, a partnership, it's hard. Not every day, but a lot of days. You fight, you disagree. But that doesn't mean you kick the woman you love out of your home, much less your town. You should have fought for her and you know it."

"She wanted to go to Denmark," I say weakly, knowing that's not exactly true.

"Bullshit," Keaton curses, and all three of our heads swing his way.

My big brother has to be mighty pissed at me to let a curse fall out of his mouth.

"You're in love with her, and she's in love with you. So you two have some issues, who cares? Presley and I couldn't be more different, but we make it work. Because we would rather die trying than be with anyone else. And at the end of the day, you and Ryan are more alike than anyone I've ever known. I knew it from the moment I saw you two together. The connection you have is deep, maybe deeper than any one of us has with our wives."

Apparently, they aren't even going to let me defend myself. Not that I really have a leg to stand on, most of what they're saying is right on the money. I hang my head, thinking about how much I fucked up. I never should have let her go. I should have gotten right in her face, challenged her like she always challenges everyone else. I should have told her to hell with her boss, we'd fight a lawsuit together. That I wanted her right here, living in our apartment and teaching in the school I know she loved working at.

"Speak for yourself," Bowen grumbles, but Forrest elbows him to get with the program. "They're right, bro. You're a moron. But you don't have to remain one."

"What does that mean?"

They all roll their eyes at me, but Forrest speaks. "Pull your head out of your ass and go get her."

Keaton follows that harsh directive up. "Go to Denmark, Fletch. Your clock is done, there is nothing keeping you here. Of course, we want you to stay, but your place is with Ryan. Plus, I always knew this town was too small for you. Knew it the minute you came home from the hospital and wailed your lungs out every time Mom brought us down to Main Street. You've spent a lot of time holding yourself back, keeping yourself small. Time to go big, brother."

Each one of them looks at me expectantly, and I know it's inevitable.

Whether it's right now, or I get my ass in gear a month from now, there is no question that I'll be going after her. And I've wasted enough time in my life.

So I ask for the help they're clearly offering. "How fast can we book a flight to Copenhagen?"

38

I stare at the picture on Presley's Instagram feed, the one she just posted.

It's a photo of Fletcher, looking as handsome as ever, standing below the monstrous clock tower. The one he designed. I missed it, the unveiling. His biggest accomplishment, the thing he's been working so hard for, and I wasn't there. The hard truth rips me apart.

Tears well behind my eyes, and I blink them back rapidly. I've cried more in the last two weeks than I ever have in my life, and I'm not about to break down in hysterics at my desk.

Not that anyone would care. Most of the people at this private security company are so secretive, they barely even look my way. They have whispered conversations in Danish, and I'm regarded like an intruder even though I'm building their entire damn threat protection system.

This job sucks balls. It's boring and easy, and I hate Copenhagen with its bike-friendly lanes and cute little riverboats. It's too damn charming and I'm too damn heartbroken.

I still want to throttle Geralyn, and I've told her as much. I gave my notice, effective immediately after the end of this project. She's been a good boss, but she soured our relationship the minute she threatened me with a lawsuit. That, and I don't take orders from anyone in that way. I'm a free bird, and she wants to tie me down. That's no *bueno* in my book, and I'm going my separate way after I build this system for these assholes.

Presley has called me a couple of times in the last two weeks, though we've avoided the subject of Fletcher. I know she's in a tough spot, but it seems she's taking my side in things. Sure, I froze up about his sobriety and got defensive when he didn't immediately agree to uproot his life and come to Denmark ...

But, he told me to leave. Basically kicked me out and told me he didn't want me around anymore.

Inside my chest, a gavel of sorrow slams down on my heart.

Fletcher was the man I was supposed to spend my life with, and it was over. I had no idea where to go from here.

Before, when I'd broken up with a guy, I'd been sad most times ... but I knew I'd get over it. That there would be another, that someone better was out there for me.

Yes, we had our underlying issues, and it would have been difficult to move past them, but it's all I wanted to do.

Because I knew that there wouldn't be another. There was no one else better.

I met my match, and he let me go. That thought was so devastating, I had to tiptoe around it in my brain. It was like laying my hand on a white hot stove; I knew I had to gingerly grasp the idea, but splaying my palm wide on it would burn me down to the core.

And it wasn't just Fletcher that I left. As much as I thought it wasn't possible, I'd made a life in Fawn Hill. I got to see my best friend every day, especially when she was struggling through her infertility issues. For the first time in forever, I was part of a group, even if it was just as a girlfriend and not as a permanent member. I had a job I really liked, and I had to put in my resignation without even saying goodbye to my students. The whole thing devastated me, and I was a little shocked that I missed waking up in that rural Pennsylvania town.

Every day for the last fourteen days, I thought about going back. About flying to Fawn Hill and demanding he take me back, because I was in love with him and I knew he was in love with me. In any other situation that I really wanted to fight for someone, I probably would.

But that was the difference here, wasn't it? Fletcher was the only man who ever truly had the power to wreck me.

And he'd done it. So, I couldn't go back.

"Can you tell me how to get to this street?"

I point to a paper map, speaking loudly, as if the guy I'm talking to is deaf.

"Yes, just take a left down this street and it's two blocks up," he says in perfect English, an amused smile on his face.

He pinned me for exactly what I am ... an idiot American tourist.

"Thank you." I nod, and speed walk off in the direction he's pointed me in.

Not that I have any idea if he's messing with me or not. I have absolutely no international travel experience, am roaming the street of a foreign country on four hours of sleep, had thrown up no more than two hours ago on my first flight ever, and couldn't read anything in Danish.

But I'm here, and I am determined to get to my woman.

Forrest worked his computer whiz magic and booked me a flight to Copenhagen a mere sixteen hours after the clock unveiling. Penelope had thrown together my suitcase, while Mom tucked an extra fifty bucks in my pocket ... for what, I'm not sure. Maybe a bag of pretzels on the plane?

Not that I could eat. I've been sweating bullets the entire time, nauseous and anxious as I've ever been. Flying is fucking scary, how come no one ever told me that?

I tried to picture Ryan's face the entire time and even snuck into my dirty memories to dream up that luscious body in front of me. That had kind of done the trick, and I'd drifted into turbulent sleep with thoughts of her perfect ass dancing in my head.

The directions Bowen had printed up on how to get to her office once I made it to the center of Copenhagen were completely wrong. I've been hopelessly wandering around for forty-five minutes, looking for some building with the name of the company she's working on a project for. Not that the city isn't beautiful, and I definitely want to explore when we're all made up and have spent a couple of hours in bed ... but I just want to get to her.

Finally, I spot it, the tall white building looking like some modern cube with windows that bubbled out from the concrete sides of it. I nearly get run over by three bikers as I try to cross the street, and I wonder again what this country's fascination with bicycles is.

"I'm here to see Ryan Shea," I say, a little frantically, to the security officer sitting behind the check-in desk.

The lobby is cavernous, with white marble everywhere, and the Dwayne Johnson lookalike, with bleach blond hair, eyes me suspiciously.

"Who?" he asks in a thick Danish accent.

I try to calm down, but he's the only thing in the way of telling my girl that I love her.

"Ryan Shea. She's working on a project for this company, as a consultant. Something about coding a system."

Again the guy looks at me like he might slam my face into the marble check-in desk, or as if I might be carrying a hidden grenade. After a few beats, he picks up the phone and rambles something off in his native language.

"What did you say your name was?" he asks me.

I didn't, which is probably why he's looking at me so strangely, now that I think about it. "Fletcher Nash."

He repeats my name into the phone and then says something else in Danish, and then hangs up.

Drumming my fingers on the desk, I search his face for any sign that she's going to come down. "Well?"

"Back away from the desk, sir. You can sit on that bench over there." The way he says it, it's not a request.

Either I go sit down, or he's going to break my arm or something. Stepping back, I pull my big duffel farther up my shoulder. I didn't even bother booking a hotel when I left, thinking I'd just find something when I touched down in the city. Or, hopefully ... I could stay with Ryan.

It all hung in the balance.

An elevator dings, and out she steps, her black locks piled on her head and a leather skirt cinching her waist. Fuck, why did she always have to wear leather? It really distracts me from every other thought I was trying to push out of my head.

"Fletcher?" Her jaw about drops to the floor. "I thought someone was fucking with me when they said you were down in the lobby. Wha ... what are you doing here?"

I stand, suddenly feeling very awkward. Especially in front of The Rock here, who has this snide smile on his meathead face.

"Can we talk outside?" I throw my head in the direction of the door.

Ryan walks out before me, looking confused, shocked, and worried at the same time. The minute the revolving door lets us out onto the sidewalk, she turns to me.

"What are you doing in Denmark?" I think she might try to touch my arm, just to make sure this isn't an illusion.

Ducking my head so that I can look her directly in the eyes, I shoot her straight. "I came here for you. To tell you that I'm in love with you, and I'm never letting you leave again."

Ryan blinks, her caramel eyes trying to comprehend. "You didn't let me leave. You told me to go."

It's an arrow to my heart, but one I deserve. "And I'm a fucking idiot, Ryan. I never should have said that. I was being a coward. I've never experienced anything outside of my hometown, it's all I know. But the woman I love was asking me to go on the adventure of a lifetime with her, and I should have said yes. I'm here saying yes, if you'll let me."

"You said you'd never leave Fawn Hill." There are tears in her voice.

"I don't care where I live, or where the hell in the world I am. Because you are my home. Nothing is right side up in my world when you're not with me. So, I came here. Can't you see? I'm addicted to you. I've been clean and sober for five years, and one look at you and I'm back on my knees, begging for just one more taste. I can't get enough of you, Ryan. You're all I think about, and when I'm with you ... you make me better."

She swings her head away, those straight, shining locks obscuring her face from me. "I promised myself, I was taking a break. I'm scared! I'm petrified to love you, but I'm also just petrified of love. I don't know how to do it, I have no clue how to receive it in a healthy way. Look at what happened when we tried!"

"Love isn't just trying one time. It's trying all the time, every single day. We let our problems overshadow everything else, we were both wrong. I'm here telling you that I want to give it all up for you. My security blanket, the safety of Fawn Hill. I thought it was the only thing that would help me stay sober ... but I don't need it anymore, I was lying to myself. You're what I need."

I'm pleading with her, and finally, I take her hands in mine. "I love you, Ryan Shea."

Now the tears spill over her lower lids. "I love you, too. I've been so miserable, Fletcher. Leaving you ... it proved that I never really loved anyone before. The way I feel about you—"

"It's something you only get once." I have to cut her off, tell her that I feel the exact same way. "So, let's stop wasting time."

She accepts by stepping into me and grabbing me behind the neck to pull my mouth to hers. All of my favorite things about her rush in; her scent, the way her lips part for me, the shape of her body in my hands.

The beat of my heart for only her.

"I can't believe you got on a plane and flew to Denmark." She breaks our kiss, laughing through her tears.

Pressing my forehead to hers, I relish the feel of her in my arms. "Believe me, it was not pretty. Don't expect me to get on one anytime soon."

Those amber eyes gaze into mine. "Guess you're stuck here with me, then."

"That was the whole point." I nuzzle her nose with mine.

"So, what now?" Ryan breathes, neither of us moving to detach our embrace.

I know the perfect answer.

"Forever."

EPILOGUE

FLETCHER

Five Years Later

The plane lands smoothly on the runway, one that was paved two years ago.

My hand is clasped tightly around hers, mostly because she knows I don't like takeoff or landing, but also because there is never a time I don't want to be touching her.

The scenery outside the window looks exactly the same as it always has. Since the day I was born, I've seen the same trees, landscape, and people. But that all changed when she stepped into my world. Or rather, when she stepped out of it.

"You happy to be home?" Ryan turns to me, her newly cut jet-black waves billowing around her shoulders.

She'd kept it long for our wedding, the tendrils of it almost skimming her waist, but immediately after, she hacked it off to what she calls a long bob. The style resembles the one she wore when we first met, all those years ago when Presley was marrying Keaton.

My ear to ear grin must give away my excitement. "Yeah, I really am. Although, Forrest is still pissed he didn't get to throw me a bachelor party. Not that any of my brothers really had one, so I don't know why I was supposed to be the one to provide the stripper-fest."

My wife chuckles. "Because your twin is jonesing for some time away from the kids. Penelope said the boys are really getting to that reckless age, and Forrest wants to keep a tight leash."

I can't believe that Travis is now seventeen, almost ready to graduate high school. And with Matthew just starting his freshman year, that left Ames at the pre-teen age of eleven, which also isn't easy. So, I guess I couldn't blame my brother.

"Very true. But it will be nice to see everyone." I pick our interconnected hands up and kiss the back of hers.

It's been a while since we've been back in Fawn Hill. After Ryan quit her job upon the competition of the Copenhagen project, about two months after I'd flown out to win her back, she decided to completely change her career. Now, she runs one of the largest nonprofit STEM training programs for kids in the world. My wife, the superstar, badass hacker, just flying around the world to teach the next generation of little coders. I'm so proud of her, but more importantly, she's so fucking happy doing her job. It's a sight to see.

We bounce around from country to country depending on which branch of the nonprofit needs help or re-vamping at the time, and we just spent almost six months in Madrid. Yes, I miss my family and my hometown, but seeing the world isn't a bad trade. It's actually pretty damn cool, and of course, I get to be with Ryan.

Someday, I know we'll settle down, move back to Fawn Hill and live in the country. But right now, it's her time. My job is flexible; I started my own woodworking business after settling in Denmark. I make smaller pieces, since I can't outfit a studio in every city we move to, but I make do and have made friends in a lot of international places. I work out of other's spaces and do what I love ... I have no reason to complain.

"They're going to try to make a big fuss about this wedding reception." She rolls her eyes, but in a good-natured way.

To say my mother was upset about our elopement would be an understatement. Not that she doesn't love Ryan, but the minute I finally convinced Ryan to marry me, I wasn't about to wait a year planning a wedding. We tied the knot two weeks ago on a beach in Madrid, and it was exactly what we wanted.

We've had discussions over the last five years about how we didn't know if marriage was right for us. Yes, we knew we'd be together for life, but Ryan wasn't keen on marriage. Argued that it was just a piece of paper, and I didn't really give a damn about a wedding. But then I'd been fooling around with making some wooden jewelry and thought wearing a wedding ring would suit me well. So I started bugging her, and it took a good eight months to convince her to get married.

"Let them. It means free food and they'll be happy about it." I nuzzle my face into her hair as the small crew at the Fawn Hill airport begins to open the plane door.

We soothed Mom's bruised ego by allowing her to throw a wedding party in our honor.

"I love you, husband. I have to admit, I like the sound of it." Ryan gives me a sassy wink.

We exit the plane, ready to haul our bags to the car, when a dull roar greets us on the grass in front of the hangar that serves as the airport.

Our entire family stands there, cheering and holding a banner that reads, "Welcome Home Newlyweds!"

Keaton and Presley's four-year-old son, Maxwell, comes bounding towards me, as my oldest brother pushes his one-year-old twin daughters in their double stroller. They ended up doing in vitro fertilization for both of their pregnancies after trying with no luck. There had been some rough patches, one time Keaton had broken down to me on the phone, but they finally got the family they wanted.

Ryan slams into Presley, their hug going on for minutes, each one half-yelling about how much they miss the other. I hug my oldest brother and then move along the crew, fist-bumping Penelope's boys and then hugging my twin brother while kissing Penelope on the cheek. Mom envelops me in a bear hug, wiping her eyes more than once, and then I greet Lily with a hug and smile.

Bowen stands next to her holding their son, Jeremy, who is three. Molly, now a smart aleck at six, throws me a peace sign and sticks out her tongue.

"We missed you all so much," Ryan gushes, and by the emotion in her voice, I know she really means it.

For as much as she tries to play the lone wolf, she's come to love my family just as much as I do. And they love her.

"Let's get going, we've got ribs in the smoker. And Hattie is baking her famous raspberry pies." Forrest rubs his stomach.

I'm amazed when Travis gets behind the wheel of one of the cars, while everyone divides into their other vehicles. I take Mom's keys as she gets into the passenger seat of her car, and Ryan takes the back seat.

"It's good to be home." I breathe, taking in the air of my hometown.

Mom palms my cheek. "It's good to have you home. Our family feels complete now."

She glances in the rearview mirror at Ryan, and I know she means more than just having us back in town.

As I start the car and pull out onto the country road back into Fawn Hill, I think about how long it took to convince my wife to marry me.

Now, how long do you think it will take to wear her down about kids?

After five years together, I've come to know Ryan *very* well. I think I can find a move or two to *do* the trick.

Looking in the rearview, I smile knowingly at my wife. Before her, I was only keeping my head above water.

With her, I am flying ... but only if she holds my hand.

Have you read <u>Fleeting</u>**? Here is a sneak peek of book one in the Nash Brothers series! Without further ado, the first chapter of Presley and Keaton's story ...**

Chapter 1

Presley

"This is probably the most embarrassing doctor's visit I've ever had. And it's not even for me."

Looking down at my grandmother's four-year-old dog, Chance, I try to give him my best stink-eye. It's a well-trained expression of mine, and it must work, because his big brown eyes, at least, hold some guilt as he drags his butt on the ground.

I have to physically pull him up the brick steps by his leash and onto the porch of the veterinarian's office, which doesn't look like an office at all. The building that houses the pet doctor is a Victorian home, with maroon shutters and dark blue whimsical trim that makes it look more like an old-school carousel than a place to treat sick animals.

The bell over the door jingles as I turn the antique brass knob to the front door, and I'm greeted by the smell of fresh cotton and lingering dog hair.

A pretty, older woman with gray hair in floral scrubs sits behind a white-washed desk, her hands flying over a keyboard as she talks to someone on the other end of the phone.

"Dr. Nash has a surgery tomorrow, but he can come up and see the horse on Thursday. Just keep at it with a lot of water, and if you don't see improvement, you know the after-hours number. All right, you too, Martha. Okay, thanks, see you then."

She looks up at me after finishing the note on her screen and smiles. A genuine, pearly-white grin ... to me, a complete stranger. It's something I haven't gotten used to in the three weeks I've been living in Fawn Hill, Pennsylvania. The rural *niceness* of this community is so foreign to my New York City mindset. You can't pull a girl out of six years of living among urbanites who are rude on arrival and expect her to take genuine caring at face value.

"Hi, there, how can I help you?" She looks down at Chance, the boxer practically frowning at her. "Oh, Chance, dear, we meet again. You must be Presley, Hattie McDaniel's granddaughter. It's nice to meet you."

Her steamrolling of the conversation catches me off guard. That's the other thing about living in a small town, everyone knows who you are and who you're related to, even if they've never seen your face.

"Uh, hi. Yes, Chance here … he ate something he shouldn't have, and I think it's … stuck. I called about twenty minutes ago." My face heats even though I don't mention exactly *what* he swallowed.

"Oh, yes, dear, I forgot! We've had such a busy morning. A horse is sick up at the Dennis' barn, and just this morning Dr. Nash has seen two cats with incontinence issues, and a rabbit with a broken tooth. It sure is a funny farm around here!"

I'm not sure what to say to this, and Chance whimpers where he sits next to me. "So, can the doctor see him?"

The receptionist stands from her desk, still smiling. "Of course, Chance is a frequent flyer. It'll be another minute or two. I'm Dierdra, by the way. Gosh, I'm sure glad you came to town to help your grandmother. With her sight, it's a wonder she's been able to keep the shop going."

I get the feeling that Dierdra is a bit of a gossip, but a well-meaning one. "Thank you, yes, I'm glad I could move here to help her."

"Have you eaten at Kip's Diner, yet? Best pie in this part of the state although it's a bit of a hidden gem. The whole of Fawn Hill is, really."

She laughs jovially, and I feel myself warming to her. She might be a bit chatty, but her kindness puts me at ease. And she's right, because since I've been here, I realized I needed a bit of Fawn Hill medicine.

Not that we'd visited a lot growing up, because Dad moved away from his hometown right after high school and didn't look back. But the two times we'd made the trip from Albany to Grandma's house for Christmas, I'd marveled at the storybook community she lived in. Fawn Hill was the quintessential small town, a gem of farmhouses and Victorian homes situated on either side of Main Street. The backdrop of the Welsh Mountains dotted the skyline, and the children here still walked to the singular elementary, middle, and high schools the town boasted.

It was picturesque, quiet living, and it wasn't a mystery what my grandmother loved so much about it. Even if I missed the bustle of the city, I could appreciate Fawn Hill for its charm.

"I haven't yet, but now I'm going to wrangle my grandma into buying me a slice of apple." I nod at her.

Chance excites when another owner walks through the door with a small, tan dog. I have to brace myself as he almost pulls my arm out of its socket and barking ensues.

Behind me, a door clicks shut, and Dierdra is talking to someone as I try to rein in Chance.

"Presley, Dr. Nash will see Chance now."

A lock of my hair is caught in my mouth as I finally turn, breathing hard with the leash looped seven times around my wrist so I can keep my grandmother's mongrel from friendly attacking the other patients.

"Come on in."

Holy crap. Why didn't anyone warn me that Fawn Hill also

had the hottest veterinarian I've ever seen? Talk about a hidden gem.

A tall drink of water with dirty blond hair, eyes the color of my favorite dark chocolate swirled with caramel, muscled thighs that couldn't possibly belong to a doctor and a smile that could charm the pants off of Simon Cowell.

Okay, I'd been watching too much *America's Got Talent*.

"You're Dr. Nash?" My voice held a tone of skeptical rudeness, and I cringed at myself. "You just ... look so ... young."

What I'd meant to say was hot ... *you're way too hot to be a vet.* This guy had sex hair, the kind you grabbed onto while he slowly stoked your fire. He looked straitlaced, a little too good-boy for my taste, but with those chiseled cheekbones and cleft chin, a girl would be blind not to feel that familiar tingle south of the border when he turned those mocha eyes on her.

But instead of the word sexy, I'd said the word young instead, and now he was giving me an amused raised eyebrow.

And then I remembered why I was here.

Oh my God. This gorgeous specimen is going to be responsible for pulling my hot pink lace underwear out of this damn dog's butt.

Click here to read Fleeting, book one in the Nash Brothers series, now!

Read the rest of the Nash Brothers series, available now!

Do you want your **FREE** Carrie Aarons eBook?

All you have to do is <u>**sign up for my newsletter**</u>, and you'll immediately receive your free book!

ALSO BY CARRIE AARONS

Standalones:

Love at First Fight

Nerdy Little Secret

That's the Way I Loved You

Fool Me Twice

Hometown Heartless

The Tenth Girl

You're the One I Don't Want

Privileged

Elite

Red Card

Down We'll Come, Baby

As Long As You Hate Me

All the Frogs in Manhattan

Save the Date

Melt

When Stars Burn Out

Ghost in His Eyes

On Thin Ice

Kissed by Reality

The Callahan Family Series:

Warning Track

ABOUT THE AUTHOR

Author of romance novels such as The Tenth Girl and Privileged, Carrie Aarons writes books that are just as swoon-worthy as they are sarcastic. A former journalist, she prefers the love stories of her imagination, and the athleisure dress code, much better.

When she isn't writing, Carrie is busy binging reality TV, having a love/hate relationship with cardio, and trying not to burn dinner. She's a Jersey girl living in Texas with her husband, daughter, son and Great Dane/Lab rescue.

Please join her readers group, Carrie's Charmers, to get the latest on new books, as well as talk about reality TV, wine and home decor.

You can also find Carrie at these places:
Website
Facebook
Instagram
Twitter
Amazon
Goodreads